D0919702

DISCARDED

DISCARDED

RENEGADE ROUNDUP

Burt Craig was riding with the wolves, and he didn't much like the company. He'd joined that bandit gang in the hope of getting back his own stake—and so far all he'd got was the chance to ride in another holdup, maybe stop lead, or get hung out of hand if he got caught. Who'd ever swallow a story that he'd only thrown in with the renegades just to check their workings and recover his own stolen dinero? No one around Cushman, for sure, not when sheriff was the gang's ringleader!

RENEGADE ROUNDUP

Tom West

GUNSMOKE

This hardback edition 2008
by BBC Audiobooks Ltd
by arrangement with
Golden West Literary Agency

Copyright © 1969 by Fred East.
All rights reserved.

ISBN 978 1 405 68206 0

British Library Cataloguing in Publication Data available.

Printed and bound in Great Britain by
Antony Rowe Ltd., Chippenham, Wiltshire

I

LIKE A yellow, dust-shrouded tortoise, the westbound Overland stage crept across the lonely immensity of rocky mesas and sweeping plateaus that was New Mexico, over yucca flats into Arizona Territory. The three passengers slumped on the worn leather seats inside were too numbed by heat-soaked monotony to give a hoot.

By the off rear window sprawled a rawboned rider with flat-planed features, ridged by high cheekbones. Opposite, a linen-dustered drummer lumped on the cushions. At the further end of the seat sat a squarish man of solid build, with shrewd eyes set in craggy features. He was garbed in a shiny broadcloth suit, with a bulge under the left armpit that might have been due to the presence of a hideaway.

Outside, on the box, boots braced against the footboard, the shaggy-bearded driver, features tanned to the hue of mahogany, yelled an occasional imprecation at a lagging leader. Beside him, feet planted on a long, flat box, the Wells Fargo guard slacked, dozing, a double-barreled ten-gauge shotgun cradled loose in his arms.

Ahead, the flats erupted into gaunt, scarred-looking hills, brownish-red in color and shadowed by dark canyons. Gradually, the plain began to undulate into rolling swales, then into spiny hills and broken arroyos. The parallel ruts that marked the track began to weave upward.

The whiskered driver nudged the man dozing beside him in the ribs. The guard, a grizzled old-timer with sun-blasted features, thick dust coating his long, drooping moustache, came awake on the instant.

"Mesquito Hills," grunted the driver and shifted his chaw. Easing the shotgun into a handier position, the other nodded. Tautly alert, eyes slitted against the sun's glare, he restlessly probed the ringing wilderness. His knobby knuckles showed white as he gripped the shotgun.

Iron-shod hooves slipping and striking sparks as the trail twisted upward through a waste of eroding rock, the six-horse team slowed to a nodding walk and, behind it, the unwieldy stage bumped and lurched.

Inside the stage, the three passengers stoically continued to endure dust and heat. Beside the rear window, Burt Craig, the rawboned rider, eased the weight of a heavy money belt that itched above his thighs. Strapped tight, it galled the skin, already prickly from sifting dust, but to Craig that itch was a pleasant reminder of the ranch he was buying outside Cushman, not too far ahead now. $3,600 in gold—one hundred and eighty beautiful double-eagles—weighted that belt. Six years' gatherings, he pondered, six years of sweat: brush popping south of San Antone; bronco busting on the Pecos; ramroding herds up the Chisholm Trail. But the payoff sure was sweet. Not bad for a button orphaned in a Kiowa raid before he was knee-high. In short, Burt Craig was one Texan who was riding high, wide and handsome.

Back in San Antonio they claimed that once he froze onto a notion he'd stick to it closer than a mustard plaster. Maybe his persistency came from the streak of Injun in him, the legacy of a paternal granmaw. In appearance, the moccasin in his ancestry left no apparent trace beyond the slightly prominent cheekbones. His loose-jointed form touched six feet in height and his lean features were bronzed by the searing heat of the plains. The belligerence of an aggressive jaw was tempered by a quizzical amusement that lingered in his slate gray eyes. Either way, at twenty-two, he was about to cash in.

The vicious spang of a Winchester punched into the passengers' ears. Harness jingled and the stage jerked to an abrupt stop as the foot brake took hold.

"Stick up, b'Gawd!" exclaimed the drummer. Craig straightened in his seat, cold premonition icing his spine. The possibility of losing that hard-earned stake under the threat of a gun had never entered his mind. Impulsively,

6

his right hand dropped to the smooth butt of the Colt holstered at his side. Before he could jerk the weapon, a man's head and shoulders were framed in the open window of the door. A faded red bandanna draped the intruder's features below eye level. Above the bandanna, two hard eyes regarded the startled passengers from behind the black muzzle of a leveled Colt.

"Step out, gents, and no shenanigans," he grated, and flung the door wide open.

From beyond the opposite door, another voice cut in, with surly emphasis, "Rattle your hocks!" Craig's head slewed around, to focus a second masked bandit. Reluctantly, his hand dropped away from the gun. With dour resignation, he rose, swung down onto the foot plate into the white blaze of the sun. The outlaw wearing the red bandanna mask, a squatty fellow, backed cautiously, eyes restless, .45 leveled, as Craig's fellow passengers followed and the three lined silently against the dust-plastered coach.

"Reach!" snapped the squatty outlaw, gesturing with his gun. Three pairs of arms pushed shoulder-high.

Craig's head swiveled as he surveyed his surroundings, desperately figuring the chance of a break. With leadened heart he realized that there was no acing out of this jackpot.

Hunched over on the box was the Wells Fargo guard, right arm clutching a spreading stain on his left shoulder. His double-barreled shotgun lay where it had dropped, against the footboard.

Jaw working angrily on his chaw, the bearded driver sat unmoving, glaring straight ahead, the lines wrapped around his gnarled wrists.

Sight of the slain guard stirred faint hope in Craig's mind of salvaging his stake. It was plain, he told himself, that the object of the holdup was the Wells Fargo box. Maybe these bandits wouldn't even bother to search the passengers. Tension easing a trifle, he gave attention to the outlaws. There were four—all masked—and they acted as though they knew their business. One, Winchester carelessly slanted in the direction of the driver, lounged by the leaders' heads. Another, wire-thin, bitter eyes gleaming above the concealing bandanna, stood to one side, silently watching the proceedings. Craig tagged him as the leader. Then there was the squatty bandit holding them under his .45 and a bull of a man in faded hickory shirt and dirt-slick denims slouching around the rear boot. This last outlaw yanked off his shapeless felt hat, lumbered up to the paunchy drummer at the far end of the line. "Donate!" he grunted.

The drummer darted a frightened glance at the squatty bandit with the leveled gun, pushed back his linen duster, fumbled in a pants pocket, dropped a wallet into the crown of the hat. To this he added a heavy silver watch whose chain was draped across his embroidered vest, then spread his arms to indicate that was all. The massive outlaw reached with his free hand, fingering the plump drummer's pockets, and fished out a sparkling diamond ring. With a growl, he dropped the ring into the hat. His massive hand knotted into a fist. Like a sledgehammer it smashed into the drummer's pudgy features. An agonized yelp tore from the victim's throat. Mashed nose spurting blood, he reeled, hit the side of the stage, slid to the ground. Without a further glance, the outlaw proceeded to the craggy-faced passenger, who impassively donated a slim roll of greenbacks. Then the big bandit was towering in front of Craig, his squat pard now sauntering beside him.

Tight-lipped, Craig slipped off a gold ring he wore on the little finger of his right hand. He hated to lose that ring, the last remembrance he had of his parents: his mother's engagement ring, a circuit of small brilliants centers by a gleaming red ruby. He dropped the ring in the hat, was reaching for his wallet when, in a flash, flaming action erupted.

A gun thundered, almost in his ears. He spun around. The Wells Fargo guard was on his feet, swaying and clutching a smoking shotgun. Cut down by the blast of buckshot, the outlaw lounging beyond the front horses lay limp on the ground. Blindly, the guard swung toward the bitter-faced bandit. He was slow, too slow. As the shotgun wavered around, the hard-eyed rider flicked a gun from his holster.

Once, twice, it stabbed fire. The guard collapsed in a quivering heap. His form jackknifed over the footboard. Released by lifeless fingers, his weapon clattered down.

The shotgun hit the ground, bounced, came to rest almost at Craig's feet. Maybe it was sight of the weapon that triggered an outburst of the seething frustration that consumed the Texan. He launched a swift kick at the big slouch standing in front of him. Taken by surprise, the big outlaw had no time to dodge. The sharp-toed riding boot took him squarely in the groin. With a hoarse gasp he dropped the hat, clutching frantically at his belly.

In a blur of motion, Craig swung a hard uppercut at the big man's jaw, connected, grabbed for his gun and pivoted to meet the squatty outlaw, hurtling at him. Even as his .45 cleared leather, realization came to the Texan that he was a split second too late. Whirling down, the steel barrel of the outlaw's gun took him above the left ear. He dropped like a poleaxed steer.

II

THE JOUNCING of the stage jolted Craig back to consciousness. His eyelids flicked up. Bemused, he stared around, striving to figure how come he was all spraddled out on the rear cushions. The man in shiny broadcloth, Waxman, he recalled, was watching him poker-faced, while the drummer, tenderly dabbing his damaged nose with a bloodied handkerchief, spilled aggrieved talk.

As he lay fighting the searing pain in his head, recollection filtered into the Texan's mind. He fingered above his left ear, flinched when his touch stirred more pain in a bulging lump under the hair. It seemed big as an ostrich egg. Gingerly, he levered to a sitting position, slid his legs off the seat and slumped against the dusty cushions, eyes squeezed tight against the pain.

Remembrance of the money belt flashed into his mind. With both hands, he feverishly fingered his waist—and his insides shrank into an icy knot. The heavy belt had vanished.

Waxman's dry tones reached his ears. "Guess you're

9

plumb out of luck, son. When the sidewinders located that belt they acted real happy. Can't say you showed good sense packing that slew of gold through the Mesquito Hills."

"The Hills got a bad rep?" Craig was striving to think clearly, but trip-hammers wouldn't quit pounding his brain.

The craggy-faced man touched a stinker to a short black stogie. "The worst! They claim there's no more lawless stretch of country in Arizona Territory."

"Don't the sheriff have a say about it?"

"I've heard the sheriff of San Marcos County just isn't interested. There's no voters in the Mesquito Hills and transcontinental passengers don't feed the ballot box. The other angle is that the sheriff lives mighty high for what he gets paid. . . ."

"This is sure one hell of a territory!"

"It's an outrage," interjected the drummer, with high-pitched indignation. "Butterfield advertises 'Travel in comfort and safety by Overland.' Comfort!" he snorted. "Safety! We've been assaulted and robbed, a guard murdered, and you speak as though it were a trifle. I intend to take the matter up with Washington."

"That sure don't help me any," said Craig wryly.

Talk died between them. The stage had hit the downgrade. Its speed accelerated and it swayed crazily. Craig hunched, sunk in pain-wracked misery, staring through a window into floating dust. Even now it was hard to realize that in one sudden, savage slash a pack of outlaws had stripped him clean. Before he hit this renegade-infested territory, he reflected morosely, he would have been accounted well-fixed. Now he was little more than a saddle-bum, flat-broke in strange terrain. Lady Luck must sure be laughing out loud.

The Concord dropped down to a rolling plain. Ahead, willows showed verdant green against the parched flats, strung along the cutbanks of a creek that meandered across the expanse. The team slacked down from a dead run and Craig glimpsed signs of habitation.

With a rattle of harness, the stage slowed to a stop outside a long yellowing relay station. The driver's yell shrilled with excitement: "Holdup! Shotgun guard daid!"

"That old goat packs more lip than a muley cow," growled the craggy-faced passenger. "Well, gents, guess this is Wicker's Ford. Ain't much more'n a spot on the trail, but we do get to stretch our legs." He opened a door and stepped out. Craig followed, but as he emerged from the coach a spell of dizziness seized him. He stumbled. Waxman, ahead, spun around, steadied his swaying form, steered him toward a narrow band of shade at the foot of the relay station's rough adobe wall. Gratefully, the Texan sank down. Waxman squatted beside him. He said conversationally, "Guess you been plumb unlucky, son. Knowing the Hills, I dropped my big roll and watch into a boot top. You crave to lay over, I'll stake you to a bed in the hotel. The joint don't look such-a-much, but they claim it's clean. There'll be another stage through at sunup."

Craig raised his aching head. "Sure thank you, mister," he said, "but I don't crave any donations. Anyway, I figure on going right on through to Cushman."

Cushman, thought Craig ruefully; that's what his ticket said, that's where Walt Jensen's ranch awaited transfer of ownership. Dammit, why did he have to strike a snag, right at the tail end of a week-long journey? His luck had sure run sour.

The dizziness seemed to have subsided and he began to take an interest in his surroundings, not that there was much in Wicker's Ford to arouse interest. The solitary street, hoof-chopped and wagon-rutted, was no more than a widening of the trail. A handful of rock-and-adobe buildings were dumped along it, then a fringe of shacks whose tin roofs glinted bright in the sunlight, and a moldering two-story clapboard structure, labeled by a faded sign, WICKER HOTEL. That was the sum of Wicker's Ford.

Attracted by the driver's shrill yell, a scattering of men had straggled up and gathered around the stage. No one seemed excited except the driver, considered Craig. Seemed as though a holdup scarce qualified as news in Arizona Territory. Bunched around the trail-stained vehicle, a fistful of shirt-sleeved townsmen and a few straw-hatted Mexicans eyed the remains of the shotgun guard, still lumped on the box, and impassively absorbed the driver's story. Equally unconcerned, a stock tender was unhooking the sweat-plastered team. He steered the horses into a rock-walled corral, returned with the replacements, hitched up, and tossed the ribbons to the still-orating driver. He stood chewing a straw, stolidly waiting for the driver's "All aboard!"

"Reckon we're due to drift," drawled Waxman. Unthinking, Craig came quickly to his feet. A spell of vertigo seized him; he staggered, fell flat on his face.

"You're in no shape to take another beating in that doggoned stage," declared the other. "Lay over!"

"Guess I got no option," admitted the Texan, and levered to a sitting position. "I got a carpet bag in the boot."

Enduring his pounding head, he watched Waxman elbow through the onlookers and brace the driver. With plain disgust, the jehu dropped down, moved to the rear of the coach, began unlacing the leather flap that covered the boot.

Waxman dropped the bag beside Craig. "So long, son!" he said, then hesitated. "You got any message—someone waiting ahead, maybe?"

"There's not a soul on God's green earth gives a hoot whether I live or die," the Texan told him bleakly.

"Well, good luck!" He turned away, plodding back to the stage.

Propped against the adobe, the Texan watched the Concord rattle away, followed it with his eyes until swirling dust veiled it from sight.

With its departure the little settlement subsided into torpidity. Loungers who had gathered around the stage drifted away. The dust settled. Nothing moved in the glare; no one displayed any interest in the lone passenger the Overland had left behind.

Craig dipped into a pants pocket, came out with a fifty-cent piece, some small silver and two brass beer checks. *That's all there is, there ain't any more,* he thought wryly. This was one hell of a spot to be stranded, with a damaged skull and less than a dollar, but somehow his predicament didn't seem to bother him. After the calamity in the Mesquito Hills nothing seemed to matter. He glanced in the direction of the tumbledown hotel up the street. He should make a stab to reach that bed Waxman had mentioned, he figured, but somehow the effort didn't seem worthwhile. All energy and ambition had drained out of him. He felt soggy as a wet sack. Lumped against the wall, he drifted off to sleep.

When he awoke, shadow shrouded Wicker's Ford. Down the street, yellow light slanted through the windows of an adobe saloon, flowing over saddle horses tied thick at the rail. Life seemed to be stirring. Riders jogged past; the gritty hinges of a batwing squealed; laughter and loud talk drifted to his ears. Sleep seemed to have dissipated the mood of depression that had enveloped him. Time he made tracks for the hotel, he decided.

Very carefully, he came erect. Trip-hammers inside his head started pounding again, but muted down. He hefted the carpet bag and began slowly walking down the street. To his relief, the dizziness no longer troubled him.

He could pledge his gun against the cost of a room, he considered. Maybe later he could peddle the .45. It should be good for twenty, twenty-five dollars. He'd sure hate to walk around naked, but a beggar couldn't be a chooser.

In no haste, he passed lumpy adobes, pushed through a swinging door and found himself in the lobby of the clapboard hotel. Mellow light from a bracketed oil lamp bathed shabby rockers, a frayed patch of carpet, shiny brass spittoons. Through an arched doorway to his left, a long plank table was visible, neatly covered with a red-and-white checked cloth. Seemed the Wicker Hotel served meals, too, he registered.

At the further end of the lobby a dog-eared register lay on the flat top of an antiquated showcase that served as desk. Keys dangled from a board spiked to the wall behind the desk and, below the keyboard, a girl sat, busily knitting.

As he stood eyeing her, she glanced up, set aside her knitting and rose briskly.

She was likely younger than he was, Craig decided, but her features already held the stamp of stoicism that the frontier impresses upon its women. She wore a plain white shirtwaist and dark skirt. Neatly plaited, her brown hair

13

was pinned precisely around her head. Unsmiling, she stood eyeing him critically as he crossed the lobby. Strictly the no-nonsense type, he reflected, conscious of the uncompromising survey of her wide-set gray eyes, and uncomfortably aware of his two-day growth of beard and rumpled, dust-stained garb. It was a sure thing that she was no beauty, but her demeanor reflected a frank honesty, a sturdy air of self-reliance, a directness that took his fancy. The blunt appraisal of her level gaze, the firmness of her small chin, could not erase the softness of her red lips.

"Guess I need a room, ma'am," he said, dropping the carpet bag in front of the showcase.

She twirled the register around. "That will be one dollar," she announced crisply.

His lips quirked. She reminded him of a severe schoolma'am admonishing a refractory pupil.

"What if I don't have a dollar?" he countered.

"You might try the straw pile in the stage depot barn," she returned, dropped into her chair and reached for the knitting.

III

THE LOSS OF his stake, the plague of his damaged head, weariness of body and spirit, fed the flood of resentment that swept over the Texan. Seemed everyone was hellbent to push him around. "I gamble that straw pile's more comfortable than the broken-down beds in this flea-trap," he bit back.

"Try it!" she suggested calmly, and resumed her knitting.

He grabbed the handle of the carpet bag, whirled away from the desk and strode stiff-legged toward the street door. Before he was halfway across the frayed carpet, the lobby began to spin wildly around him. He teetered, recovered, crashed down . . .

When understanding returned he was lying on his back. He moved restlessly and bed springs creaked. His eyes blinked open. Nearby, a glass-bowled lamp sat on a scratched bureau. Its light revealed a washstand, a discolored mirror, and a china washbowl perched on a straightback chair beside the bed. His gunbelt and his pants dangled across the back of the chair.

The brown-haired girl, a dripping towel in one hand, stood eyeing him anxiously.

He struggly to sit erect, but the girl reached and firmly restrained him. "Lie still!" she directed in a tone that admitted of no argument. "You may have a concussion."

He lay eyeing her belligerently, enduring the pounding in his head. The girl wrung out the towel, reached and carefully draped it over his forehead, smoothing the ends back over his ears. It felt cool and infinitely refreshing.

"How come you're doctoring me?" he challenged. "You got no use for deadbeats."

Ignoring his question, she said, "There'll be a stage in the morning. You'll only have to endure our broken-down beds for tonight." Adroitly, she spread a blanket over him, stepped to the bureau and turned the wick of the lamp low. She checked, eyeing the Texan's furious features with a faint smile. "You won't be alone, Mr. Craig; you'll have the fleas for company." With that, she tip-tapped out of the room.

Narrow shafts of sunlight, knifing through rents in the window shade, crisscrossed the room when Craig awoke. His head felt as though it was chockful of molten lead, but otherwise, he decided, he was as spry as a two-year-old. His boots were neatly arranged by the far wall and his hat hung from a peg. He threw the coverings aside and swung his legs off the bed. Then he became aware that his pants were missing from the chair. He hastily grabbed a blanket when quick steps sounded on the bare boards of the passage outside. The girl, packing a metal tray covered with a white napkin, came through the doorway. She nodded briefly in his direction, jerked up the window shade with one hand, hooked a rung of the straightback chair with the toe of a high-button shoe, yanked it up beside him and set the tray on it.

"Guess I mislaid my pants," said Craig.

"Eat your breakfast," she directed crisply, ignoring the

15

remark. Flicking off the napkin, she revealed a steaming mug of coffee, buttered toast, fried eggs.

He suddenly realized that he was as hungry as a horse and decided to defer the subject of pants. The girl moved over to the window and stood gravely watching while he vigorously cleaned up the plate. Somewhere beneath her frigid exterior she must have a heart, he reflected, downing the last of the coffee. Else why would she fix his head, give him a bed, feed him, well knowing he didn't have a dollar.

He set down his empty mug with a deep sigh of satisfaction. "Guess now I eat crow," he said with a crooked grin. "Reckon I spoke out of turn last night. Sure was feeling as sullen as a sore-headed dog. This bed now, I gamble they couldn't match it at the Ritz."

"Save your breath," she advised with cool indifference. "I had you tagged a deadbeat, drifting through. Then, when you collapsed, I realized you must be the victim of the holdup who left the stage."

"I'm still flat broke." He reached for his gunbelt. "Peddle this—the Colt should be worth twenty smackers."

"Don't you think you need a gun, for protection?" she retorted with faint mockery. "Now get back into bed and rest."

"Rest!" he echoed. "I need my pants. Heck, I'm fitter'n a coop of catbirds."

"You get your pants tomorrow, maybe," she returned with unsmiling finality. Ignoring his exasperated glare, she picked up the tray and headed for the door. It struck Craig that he'd waste words arguing. With a shrug, he rolled back onto the mattress; his head did seem to be acting up again.

Left alone, Craig lay considering the events of the previous day. First thing to do, he cogitated, when that ornery female delivered his pants, would be to contact Jensen and break the news that the deal for the ranch was off. Then he'd have to get busy and earn some dinero to settle his hotel bill.

Twice more that day the obdurate Miss Wicker fed him, composedly ignoring insistent demands for his pants.

16

However, when she brought up his breakfast the following morning they were slung over a rounded arm.

"How's the head?" she inquired briskly.

"Fine!" he asserted.

"There was no fracture, just that awful bruise," she murmured, eyeing him thoughtfully. "I suppose it's safe to allow you on your feet." She dropped the pants on the bed. "Now don't overdo it!" she admonished severely.

"Sure won't—doc," he assured her with a grin. "Reckon I'll hit for Cushman."

"Not until you're fit to travel," she decreed firmly, and reached for the pants. Craig grabbed them. "Now listen," he begged. "I'm as right as rain and maybe I should set you right as to how things are." He told of his deal to buy the Jensen spread, the holdup that blew his plans sky-high.

Perched on the edge of the bed, the girl listened gravely, sympathy reflected in her gray eyes. "So now," concluded the Texan, "I start from scratch. After I break the bad news to Jensen, I figure on hunting me a hole in a spread and earning the wherewithal to pay you off. Anyway, I'm through setting. Where can I pick up a stage?"

"The Overland went through an hour back," she pondered. "There won't be another westbound stage for two days. There's a dun in the shanty barn out back, eating its head off. Do you think you could ride?"

"Ma'am, I can top anything I can clap a saddle on," he assured her, in high good humor at the prospect of action. Lips quirking, he added, "Ain't you scairt I'll keep riding plumb out of the Territory?"

She studied him soberly. "No," she decided, then added with a tight smile, "It's customary around here to hang horse thieves."

Craig was yanking on his boots when he heard heavy steps clomping down the corridor outside. The door opened and Waxman's solid form lumped in the doorway.

"How you feeling?" he inquired, plumping down on the chair.

"Spry as a two year old," Craig told him. "I'd of been on my feet before but the ornery female who runs this joint grabbed my pants."

"Could be she showed good sense," commented the other, and stuck a stogie between his lips. Unexpectedly, he fired a question: "Figure you could identify them outlaws?"

"Maybe," returned the Texan doubtfully. "You got a line on 'em?"

"Not yet," admitted Waxman, puffing his smoke. "Hashed it over with Sheriff Pomeroy in Cushman. Pomeroy's mighty bothered by these holdups; they don't help his rep."

"How come you're on the prod?" inquiried Craig curiously. "Didn't you hang onto your roll? The drummer, now, was squawking like a stuck pig."

Without speaking, his visitor pulled a small metal badge from a vest pocket, held it toward the Texan. It was engraved, *Tom Waxman. Pinkerton. #413*

"Butterfield's bothered," he explained, "so they rung us in to clean things up." He heaved to his feet, raised a hand in farewell. "Wal, I got to drift. See you around."

Craig liked the looks of the dun, a blocky animal with muscular shoulders, small head and intelligent eyes. It looked speedy, with plenty of bottom. He smoothed a blanket across the straight back, cinched on a stock saddle that sat on a rack, adjusted the oxbow stirrups.

When he rode out of the barn, the dun essayed a few playful crowhops, then settled down to a steady jog trot. Happy that he had shucked the giddiness and exalting in the feel of a horse beneath him, Craig followed the deep-rutted stage road.

It was near noon when he rode into the yard of Jensen's Box J. *Sure is a good-looking spread,* he considered, heading for the water trough. To his left lay a solid rock-and-adobe ranch house, fronted by a roofed gallery. Opposite sat a low-built bunkhouse with massive adobe walls. Other ranch buildings stood around, flat-roofed, with projecting vigas. A stout corral lay beyond the water trough, above which a windmill towered, its blades slowly spinning, impelled by a faint, sage-scented breeze.

It was a place after the Texan's own heart. If it hadn't been for a twist of fate, he reflected somberly, he would

18

have been riding in to take possession, not to confess that his status was now little better than that of a saddlebum.

Dismounting at the trough, he watered the dun and looped its reins around a post. As he paused to build a smoke, a tall man in cowman's garb stepped out of the house. His weathered features were as deep-tanned as old leather and decorated by a down-curling, sun-faded moustache. The cowman came to the edge of the gallery, looking him over with a grave and probing eye.

Scuffing dust, Craig stepped toward him. "Walt Jensen?"

"You read the brand." The cowman's voice was deep, unhurried. "You could be Burt Craig from San Antone."

The Texan nodded.

"Figured you was about due," drawled Jensen. He indicated a rocker. "Take the weight off your legs."

Craig dropped onto a seat, while Jensen sank into an adjoining rocker, stretching out long legs. His deep-set eyes weighed the visitor silently as he lifted the makin's out of a vest pocket and carefully made a cigarette.

"Might just as well break the bad news," said Craig tightly. "The deal's off."

"You don't say!" returned the cowman, with no change of expression.

"Don't nurse the idea I got cold feet," added the Texan hastily. "I was packing the down payment, riding the Overland, when road agents cleaned me in the Mesquito Hills." He touched the left side of his head with a rueful smile. "I still carry their brand."

Jensen sat drawing on his smoke, absorbing this. "Guess we got more damned outlaws in San Marcos County than honest men," he commented finally.

Both men's heads slewed around when a girl suddenly burst out of the house like a cyclone. And she was sure a sight for sore eyes, decided the Texan. Beneath a wealth of glossy black hair, her features, hued a delicate brown, were striking in their perfection. Her eyes were dark pools of smoldering fire and her lips a scarlet slash above an oval chin tilted with unconscious arrogance. She was colorfully garbed in a yellow blouse, with a bright red bandanna knotted around her neck and a fringed buckskin skirt that revealed shapely calves.

"My daughter Dolores," drawled Jensen.

As the girl dashed past them, ignoring Craig, he barked, "Dolores!" an edge to his tone.

She checked and whirled around, met the Texan's absorbed gaze with haughty disinterest, then transferred attention to her father. "Well?" Her tone was rich, pulsating, tinged with brittle impatience. At close quarters, Craig became aware of a sulkiness that marred her red lips and lines of discontent that spiderwebbed her brow.

"The gal's kinda impetuous and prickly as a chunk of cholla," the rancher volunteered apologetically. To the girl he said gruffly, "Shake hands with Burt Craig, from San Antone."

Craig rose hastily as she stepped toward him with no enthusiasm and extended a disdainful hand. Then he froze, gaze riveted on the girl's slim fingers. A ring circled one— a circlet of small brilliants, centered by a gleaming red ruby. it was the treasured ring that had been his mother's, a ring he had dropped into an outlaw's stained felt hat three days back in the Mesquito Hills."

IV

HIS MIND in a turmoil, Craig stared at the ring. It just couldn't be his, he told himself. It must be a duplicate and the resemblance a pure trick of chance. Then he remembered that one of the tiny brilliants circling the ruby on his own ring had dropped out of the setting, years before. He reached, grasped the girl's outstretched hand, leaned over it, eyes intent on the ring. One brilliant was missing! His grip tightened. Resentfully, Dolores Jensen jerked her hand free.

"Just where did you get hold of that ring, ma'am?" he inquired curtly.

"That's no business of yours," she exploded with quick resentment.

"I figure it is my business," he retorted tightly. "I donated that ring not four days back in a stage holdup." He spun around to face the rancher, right hand slapping his gun butt. "Guess you better start talking, and talking fast," he snapped.

The tall cowman straightened, stood meeting his visitor's accusing gaze imperturbably, transferred his attention to the girl, who stood glowering at Craig, indignation flaming in her dark eyes.

"Jest how you come to get holt of that bauble, gal?" he wanted to know.

"Jack Pomeroy gave it to me at the dance last night," she told him sulkily.

"And just who is Jack Pomeroy?" put in Craig.

"The sheriff!" said Jensen shortly.

If the rancher was tied up in this, thought Craig, he was sure a prime bluffer.

Jensen attempted no further explanation, just eyed his daughter, gnawing the ends of his moustache. "Gimme the ring!" he said finally. The girl's gaze locked with his. "You heard me!" he barked.

Reluctantly, she slipped the ring off her finger and handed it to him.

Jensen took it, eyed it thoughtfully. His gaze lifted and his deep-set eyes focused on Craig. "How come you're so doggone sure you owned this?" he demanded. "Could be it's a look-alike."

"It's sure as hell mine," snapped the Texan. "Take a gander inside the band. You'll find an inscription *G to M*. George Craig was my paw, Mildred Craig my maw."

Wordlessly, Jensen tilted the ring, examined it, squinting. He nodded slowly. "Guess it carries your brand," he agreed, and carelessly tossed it toward Craig.

"Dad!" protested the girl vehemently.

"Beat it!" he said shortly. For a moment, fire in her dark eyes, she seemed about to argue, then she flung away, flouncing across the yard toward the barn.

Jensen dropped onto the rocker again, began building a smoke, brow knitted. Craig stood fingering the ring, battling suspense and perplexity. If the girl spoke the truth, he cogitated, it seemed that this Sheriff Pomeroy was tied up with the renegades. But could be the rancher was running a bluff. Maybe he was working in cahoots with this outlaw outfit, passed word when a buyer was due on a westbound stage with a chunk of dinero. Maybe selling the Box J was a regular racket—to tole money to San Marcos County.

Jensen's drawling tones broke in upon his thoughts. "A mighty curious business."

"I'd say mighty crooked!" threw back Craig, eyeing the rancher narrowly.

"And it sure raises your hackles," commented the other, touching a stinker to his cigarette. "Wal, can't say I'm surprised any."

Jensen, Craig decided, was either a supreme bluffer, or his hands were clean. Maybe he should play along with the hombre.

"You figure your gal's telling a straight story?" he inquired.

"Dolores is as explosive as a firecracker, but she's no liar."

"Which points the finger straight at this Sheriff Pomeroy."

"Sure does," agreed Jensen equably, contemplating his cigarette smoke.

"You don't seem surprised any."

"There's been talk," returned the other. "Sticky-fingered politician and such."

"From where I stand it looks worse, damn sight worse," retorted Craig brittlely. "I'm wondering just where you stand."

Jensen leaned back in the rocker, gravely measuring his fuming visitor. "Mister," he said, an edge to his tone, "I figure I know jest how you feel. You're a stranger, you've been hogswiggled, you're in a mood to gore. Wal, chew on this. I never set eyes on that doggoned ring till Dolores flashed it not ten minutes back. I ain't tied in with no outlaw gang or no conniving politicians. Pomeroy's sweet on Dolores, but damned ef I can do a thing about that. Why in thunder don't you brace the hombre?"

The rancher's forthright words had the ring of truth, thought Craig; he should make dead sure before he started trouble. "Guess I'll do that very thing," he decided.

Weathered features expressionless, Jensen watched him

trudge back to the water trough, loosen the dun's reins, step into leather.

Cushman was the same as a fistful of other cow towns in Texas and New Mexico, decided Craig when his pony jogged past yellowed adobes that fringed the town and along the hoof-pocked stretch that was Main Street. False-fronted stores and saloons, mostly rock-and-adobe, drowsed in the sunglare. Saddle horses stood hipshot along gnawed hitchrails. In the shade of the canopied plankwalks drifted a scattering of long-skirted housewives, spurred punchers, swarthy Mexicans. He passed a bulky livery barn with a high-fenced wagon yard and a squat rock-fronted bank; checked his pony outside a box-like red brick building with the words SAN MARCOS COUNTY COURTHOUSE picked out across its front with yellow brick.

Neckreining the dun to the rail, he dismounted, paused to slap the dust off his pant legs with his Stetson, and mounted a broad flight of brick steps.

Inside, he checked doors till he found one JACK POMEROY, COUNTY SHERIFF. He turned the handle and stepped into a high-ceilinged room. His quick glance took in several straightback chairs spaced along the opposite wall, which was plastered with wanted notices, a row of sawed-off shotguns in a rack, and, near two narrow windows, a scratched rolltop desk. In front of it, a big man was sprawled in a swivel chair, puffing a fat cigar and perusing a newspaper. A sheriff badge gleamed on his shirt front. At the sound of the opening door he looked up and nodded amiably.

Craig jingled across the varnished floor, dropped onto a chair beside the desk. "You Sheriff Pomeroy?" he inquired.

The big man nodded and flashed the mechanical smile of an elected official. "Well," he inquired affably, "what can I do for you?"

Pomeroy seemed young for a sheriff, registered Craig, but he was sure a fine-looking figure of a man, six feet of big-boned, bland assurance. Thick blond hair curled down over his ears, his eyes were clear blue, his jowls razor-smooth and a neat moustache was dabbed over firm lips.

23

Even his garb was striking, from the black Stetson hanging from a peg to handmade riding boots that must have set him back fifty dollars. He sure looked the perfect picture of a sheriff, almost *too* good to be true, considered the Texan; perhaps the only other flaws in the lawman's make-up were an overfed look and an unconscious cockiness.

"The moniker's Burt Craig," he said, and briefly related the story of the stage holdup and loss of his money belt.

When he was through, Pomeroy exclaimed earnestly and sympathetically, "A great loss, Mr. Craig, a great loss! The Butterfield driver turned in a full report. These holdups are most regrettable, but—" he shrugged hopelessly—"what can I do with a mere handful of deputies? This is a big county and lightly settled. Renegades infest the hills." He flashed white teeth in a quick smile. "I don't need to assure you that every effort will be made to round up these miscreants and recover your stake."

"I already recovered a ring I lost," said Craig. "This ring!" He held up his right hand. As Pomeroy's glance focused on the red ruby, Craig could have sworn that a quickly disguised shock of surprise registered in the bold, brassy eyes.

"You—lost it?" The Texan detected a note of uneasiness in the lawman's hearty tone.

"Yep!" he said shortly. "I fed this ring to the kitty at the holdup, and it just turned up on a gal's finger—Miss Dolores Jensen. She claims it was a gift, from you." He paused, eyeing Pomeroy closely. For moments, tight silence held the office. Then Pomeroy's features slowly crinkled into a broad smile. "I'd say that was a real lapaloozer," he chuckled.

"I'd say something stinks," barked Craig.

The sheriff's broad shoulders shook with amusement. "It sure looks bad," he agreed, puffing complacently. "Just proves you can't tell a hoss by its coat. One of my deputies found that ring on the person of a bandit, beefed in a holdup attempt. Naturally, we assumed it was his property. Dolores is a real nice girl and she loves geegaws." He raised his shoulders. "I like Dolores, so I passed it on to her."

"You figured it was yours to give away?"

Pomeroy smiled. "The man was dead. Why not make Dolores happy? No one was robbed."

"Except me!" put in Craig bitterly.

The sheriff spread his hands. "How could I know?" he protested.

Craig sat silent, chewing the explanation over. Finally he came to his feet, forcing a smile. "Sorry to have troubled you, Sheriff. Pity the hombre your deputy beefed warn't packing my $3,600, too."

"Your luck didn't stretch that far," commiserated Pomeroy, his tone deep with feeling. "But," he added cheerfully, "we'll be looking!" He came to his feet, grabbed the Texan's hand, pumping it. "It's been a pleasure meeting you, Craig. Sure hope you'll stick around. San Marcos is a great county. All we need is people—people like you."

In no cheerful frame of mind, Craig left the courthouse, dropped down the steps. At the rail he paused, thoughtfully began to make a smoke, unable to discard a notion that there was more to the recovery of the ring than the affable sheriff had revealed. Pomeroy's explanation, he reflected had been pat, too pat. And why, when the sheriff pumped his hand at parting, had the lawman's palm been damp? Was it nervousness? Was Pomeroy hiding something behind that bluff exterior?

It could be, he thought sourly, that heists were so common in San Marcos County that lawmen took them for granted. In Texas there would have been a posse on the trail of those outlaws quicker than hell could scorch a feather. But it seemed things were different in Arizona Territory.

V

AT A LOOSE END, Craig mounted and drifted down the street. Seemed all he could do, he reflected, was head back to Wicker's Ford and return the horse. Maybe he could make a deal with Miss Wicker, pledge the ring against loan of the dun. Then he'd mosey around, hunt up a job and work himself out of debt. It was one hell of a climax to the hopes he'd nursed when he left San Antone. Lady Luck had sure slapped him down.

Sight of a paint-peeling sign nailed to the wooden canopy of a saloon, THE OLD FRUIT, reminded him that he needed to wash the dust out of his throat. He was broke, he thought humorlessly, but not flat broke: a little chicken feed still jingled in his jeans. Neckreining the dun to the rail, he tied up and ducked through the batwings.

It was mid-afternoon and business was slack. Except for the barkeep, listlessly swotting flies behind a wooden counter that spanned the rear of the saloon, the place was empty. Lithochromes of scantily-clad burlesque queens adorned the plastered adobe walls and brass kerosense lamps dangled from the squared vigas of the low ceiling. Through the open door of a small room beyond the end of the bar he glimpsed a circular poker table, surrounded by a disorder of empty chairs. Overladen ash trays spilled cigar butts and cigarette stubs onto the green baize and two empty whiskey bottles stood like sentinels among dirty glasses. *Must have been a big game last night,* he registered, dropped two bits on the bar and ordered a bottle of beer. Packing it, he scraped back a chair at a table by the dusty front window and relaxed, sipping the beer. It was warm, but it had a satisfying dampness.

His head swiveled as the batwings squealed on gritty hinges and two riders entered the saloon. He flicked a casual glance in their direction—and his attention became fixed. One was a squatty fellow, with bowed legs, unshaven jowls and restless eyes; the other a bull of a man in faded hickory shirt and dirt-slick denims. Although their features had been masked by bandannas, Craig knew on the instant that they were the pair who had looted the passengers at the stage holdup. That squatty hombre had clouted him with a gun barrel.

Debating his next move, he watched them covertly as they jingled up to the bar. Abruptly, the big man stopped, and Craig had a hunch that he had been recognized, sighted in the ornate backbar mirror. The pair stood trading low-voiced talk, then began angling toward him. Craig's right hand dropped to the butt of his holstered gun, but he checked the impulse to draw. It was loco, he told himself, to start gunplay on a hunch.

The two were close now. The burly rider, ahead, checked at the table, looking down at Craig. The Texan thought his attention quickened when he glimpsed the ruby ring.

"Mister," he growled, "me and Brazos here're dryer'n a cork leg and busted flatter'n a snake's belly. Sure would thank you to set 'em up."

The Texan shrugged. "Sorry, feller, I'm broke."

"Flashing that sparkler!" Truculence edged the burly rider's tone now. "Quit hurrahin' me, mister." He pulled out a chair and dropped into it. The rider called Brazos promptly yanked up a chair and plunked down on the Texan's left, crowding him, and boxing him in.

Craig thought fast. Trouble was brewing. It was apparent that the pair had entered the saloon hunting him. Why, he couldn't figure, unless they craved the ring. But how could they know the ring had been returned? That knowledge was confined to just three persons: Jensen, his daughter and the sheriff. A tight anger began building up in him. Not content with lifting his stake, these buzzards were itching for more trouble. Well, he'd hand them all the trouble they could digest.

"What's really itching you two?" demanded the Texan curtly.

"Hey, Jake, he wants to know what's itching us!"

"You, mister!" snapped the man called Jake, and dabbed for his gun.

Craig grabbed the edge of the table with both hands, rammed with all his strength. Before his gun had cleared leather, the table took the burly rider in the middle, spilling him backward in a flurry of arms and legs. Craig felt the squat rider, jammed against him on the chair to his left, move hastily as he fumbled for his .45. The Texan flung his left arm in a flailing back-arm blow, almost knocked the smaller man out of his seat, twisted around before he recovered his wits, and latched both hands onto his throat. Interlocked, they spilled to the floor. The squat rider was hard-muscled, tough as rawhide, but no match for the enraged Texan. All the frustration of the past few days

27

boiled up in Craig. Growling like an angry mastiff, he dug his thumbs into the other's windpipe. Choking, the squat rider fought desperately to break the grip on his throat, legs threshing and fingers clawing for his opponent's eyes. On top of the writhing form, Craig felt the other's body muscles slacken. Panting, the Texan loosened his grip, came to his feet. The squat rider lay inert, mouth gaping, chest rising and falling spasmodically.

In sudden recollection of his remaining opponent, the Texan whirled around. The big man, Jake, had levered to a sitting position and was hunched, staring around with bewildered eyes.

Craig bent, slid the squatty rider's gun out of leather, leveled it on his pard. "On your feet!" he snapped.

The burly rider blinked, then laboriously straightened, apparently still dazed. Jamming the muzzle of the purloined .45 into his belly, Craig relieved him of his gun.

The barkeep, toting a bung starter, was edging cautiously toward them. "You crave I should call a deputy?" he inquired.

"Nope!" Craig threw back. *What's the use?* he reflected. He had no concrete evidence these two hardcases were involved in the holdup. They'd deny it for a certainty. As for the ruckus, it was their joint testimony against his and they'd name him the aggressor. The struggle with the squat rider had started pistons pounding again in his damaged head and he felt strangely unsteady on his feet. He had to get out of there before he collapsed, he knew, and was again at the mercy of these vultures. He turned away and lurched toward the batwings.

Outside, shadows were beginning to finger across the the street. Teetering like a drunk, he crossed the plankwalk, tossed the renegades' guns into the street and fumbled with the reins of the dun. Main Street spun around him as he hauled into the saddle. Gripping the horn with his left hand to maintain his seat, he headed out. When the last adobe dropped behind he raised the pony to a trot, following the deep-cut ruts of the stage road across the swales. The throbbing of his head increased, seeming to keep tune with the dun's hooves as they beat a rhythmic tattoo on the

28

heat-hardened ground. In vain, he strove to think coherently, reviewing the events of the day, but they persisted in melding together, dancing in and out of his whirling brain. Finally, he quit trying to figure and slumped helplessly over the dun's withers.

VI

CRAIG awoke in full daylight, lying completely clothed on his bed in the Wicker Hotel. Still half-drugged by sleep, he sat up, staring bemusedly around. Recollection of the events of the previous day slowly began to flow into his mind, but from the time he left the saloon he couldn't remember anything. The dun must have known its way home, he pondered; he sure couldn't recollect helping any.

He padded across the room, dug razor, shaving brush and soap from the carpet bag. Stripping to the waist, he spilled water from the jug set beside the washstand into the chipped china bowl and began lathering a prickling of beard.

As he scraped, his mind was busy, reviewing his misadventures at the countyseat. A certainty began to build up that there was something almighty queer associated with the ruby ring. Nothing but that ring could have brought the two renegades into the Old Fruit, he decided, but who had toled the hardcases onto him—Sheriff Pomeroy, Walt Jensen, or Jensen's daughter?

Someone was cashing in big from lawlessness in San Marcos County and the finger pointed at Pomeroy.

But what chance had he, a stranger, to buck what was plainly an organized gang? he reflected. Likely the renegades paid off the sheriff and other officials to close their eyes and mouths. Which meant he could expect no help from the law.

Craig paced the room, toweling off. Might just as well butt his head against a brick wall as buck this outlaw outfit, he cogitated. Of a sudden, he remembered the Pinkerton man, and jerked to a stop. Here was an ally! But if Waxman had divulged his identity to the sheriff, odds were that every renegade in the county had been alerted, and the Pinkerton man's life wouldn't be worth a plugged nickel. He had to find Waxman and wise him up—fast.

Quickly, he slicked his hair down, dressed and dropped down to the dining room.

Miss Wicker dabbed into view at a rear doorway, a white apron covering her front and water dripping from her rounded arms.

"Guess my tapeworm's hollerin', ma'am," volunteered the Texan.

"Too bad!" she threw back, unsmiling. "We serve breakfast from six to eight. It's after nine now."

Craig raised his shoulders resignedly and turned away, checked as the girl spoke again. "Oh well, if you'll eat in the kitchen, I'll fix you some eggs."

"That's mighty nice of you, ma'am." He smiled.

The kitchen was hot. A large sheet-iron stove stood against one wall, a wood box beside it. Dirty dishes were heaped in the steaming water of a wooden sink, over the side of which the spout of a hand pump projected. More dishes were stacked on shelves and a variety of pots and pans hung from nails on the wall behind the stove. A small circular table stood in the center of the room and a stable lamp hung from a rafter.

"Well, how was your trip?" Miss Wicker asked as she broke four eggs into a frying pan.

"A real eye-opener," he drawled, dropping into a chair at the table. "I located a ring the holdup hombres grabbed."

"You did!" The girl swung around with quick interest.

He held up a hand, displaying the ruby.

"It's beautiful!" she breathed, and he had a notion there hadn't been much room in her life for jewelry.

"How did you find it?" she wanted to know.

He told of the events of the previous day, omitting mention of the saloon fracas.

"How fortunate!" she murmured. "This Dolores Jensen—was she attractive?"

"Pretty as a heart flush!" he declared emphatically.

"Indeed!" She turned back to the stove and became engrossed with the cooking.

"I'm kinda interested in the sheriff," he threw at her. "You acquainted with the local deputy? Maybe he'd give me the lowdown."

"Tom Farnham's out of town." Her tone held cold disinterest.

"Where would I locate his office?"

"Down the street, west of the stage depot."

She set a plate of fried eggs and toast before him, poured hot coffee. "That's the best I can manage at this hour," she said shortly.

Eating, Craig watched her as she stepped over to the sink and began to busy herself with dirty dishes. The girl was sure a glutton for work, he considered; pity she had to make a galley slave of herself running this tumbledown hotel. Fixed up, with her figure, she could be a real looker.

To make talk, he commented, "That bunch at the courthouse got the county hogtied. A man would be loco to buck 'em."

"If you can't beat them, join them," she retorted.

Craig stopped eating, froze, struck by a sudden idea. The practical Miss Wicker had hit the bull's-eye. That was the answer: smash the crooks from the inside. Work with them, wise up as to how the sidewinders operated, then hit them where it hurt. The problem was how to gain acceptance. They sure would look slant-eyed at a victim who'd just lodged a complaint with the sheriff craving to join their ranks. Then the solution hit him—with the impact of a slug.

A sun-drugged torpidity held the straggling little settlement when Craig stepped out of the hotel. The only sign of life on the sandy widening of the trail was a mongrel questing over the ruts.

Craig paused to make a smoke, then began to saunter down the street, toward the stage depot.

Separated by a brushy lot from the flat-roofed depot, with its rock-walled corral, stood a squat adobe. Along its front a warped wooden bench was set and above its doorway a faded sign carried the words DEPUTY SHERIFF.

Casually, Craig paused outside, reached and turned the

knob of the door. He was not surprised when the door opened. Here, as in Texas, few bothered with locks.

He stepped into the small, square interior and looked around. It was apparent that the local lawman was a man of simple tastes. The floor was packed earth and two blankets were neatly folded on a bunk at the far end. At the other end, beneath a glassless window, a chair with laced rawhide seat was thrust beneath a plank table littered with old newspapers, a mail-order catalog, official forms. Two wooden boxes were set on a shelf above the table, an old slicker hung from a peg, a spooled bedroll stood in a corner. A fly-specked calendar and a small heating stove completed the furnishings. Craig's forehead furrowed; he was hunting wanted notices and there wasn't one in sight.

He moved over to the shelf, lifted down one of the boxes. It was jammed with oddments of saddlery, rawhide whangs, spurs, jingle-bobs. Setting the box back, he reached for the other, and an exclamation of satisfaction left his lips. A medley of dodgers was stuffed into it, the accumulation of years, many yellowed with age.

Carrying the box to the bunk, he upended it. Crackling sheets showered out. Carefully, he began to finger through them, carefully scrutinizing each dodger before setting it aside. Finally he paused, eyeing the blurred reproduction of the head and shoulders of a wanted man who vaguely resembled himself. The dodger had been issued by a Texas sheriff some two years before. He read:

$500 REWARD
WANTED FOR BANK ROBBERY

Lester Collins. Age 22; height 6′1″; weight 165; black hair; gray eyes. No scars. Wanted for holdup of: the Lennox County Bank; First National Bank, Marlburg; Merchant's Bank of Lodestar. This man operates alone. Dangerous gunman. Send information to:

Frank Lawson, Sheriff
Lennox County, Texas.

Carefully, he folded the crackling sheet and stuffed it into a pants pocket.

VII

WHEN THE Texan stepped into the frayed hotel lobby the energetic Miss Wicker was busily wielding a broom.

"Don't you ever quit, ma'am?" he remonstrated whimsically. "You got more doggoned energy than the rest of this burg lumped together."

"Someone has to keep the place presentable," she returned defensively.

"You in a mood to dicker?"

"Dicker?" She paused, a question in her eyes, absently patting vagrant strands of hair into place.

"What's the dun worth, with its rig?"

The girl's lips pursed as she considered. "Well, I took it for a thirty-two dollar board bill," she murmured, then added quickly, "There's the feed, too."

"Forty dollars, say?"

"Quit funning!" Impatience edged her tone. "How can you buy a horse when you can't pay for a meal?"

He slipped off the ruby ring and held it out. "I'll leave this as security till I square things up."

Her glance dropped to the stone and he read longing in the steady brown eyes. "I'll trade, and wipe the slate clean," she offered, with poorly concealed eagerness.

Craig shook his head regretfully. "No, ma'am. I wouldn't part with that ring for all the cattle in Texas—but I sure need a hoss."

She sighed. "Very well, then, we'll do it your way."

He handed her the ring. She slipped it onto a finger, eyed it engrossed as she twirled her hand, so that the stone reflected light. With a start, she looked up, met his glance, flushed and hastily removed the glittering circlet. "What do you intend to do?" she asked quickly, covering faint embarrassment.

"Most anything to turn a dollar, I guess. And I'd say the job that pays best in San Marcos County is heisting."

"Quit talking nonsense!" she snapped. "And get out of here—I have work to do."

He moved toward the door, paused as he pushed it back, and sang out, "You keep good care of that ring."

"You keep good care of yourself," she replied, with a quick smile that transformed her sober features. "And don't nurse crazy ideas!"

For a second time Craig rode into Cushman. He rode the length of the street, checking for Waxman, to warn him and discuss the plan. He drew rein outside the one hotel, figuring to look there. An unexpected hail from the plank-walk caught him thinking about his next move if he didn't locate Waxman. His head swiveled and he spotted Sheriff Pomeroy's soldierly form. The sheriff beckoned. Craig stepped down and hitched the dun.

"It's sure nice meeting you again," said Pomeroy, smiling, clapping him on the back with effusive friendliness. "Figured that you'd maybe headed back to Texas."

"What would I use for dinero?" countered Craig, wondering what was behind all this cordiality.

Pomeroy's smile was expansive. "That's no problem!"

"I'm listening!" prompted the Texan.

"Dolores set her mind on that ring. All you got to do is set the price and I'll take it off your hands."

"Heck, Sheriff." Craig's tone reflected regret. "Sure sorry to disappoint the gal but I traded that ring for a hoss and saddle. Feller boarded the stage east." He read quick chagrin in the lawman's eyes.

Pomeroy caressed his dab of moustache, a quick frown clouding his features. It smoothed out and he beamed again. "So you're sticking around!" His brassy eyes regarded the Texan curiously.

"Yep. Hunting a job."

"Punching cows?"

"There's quicker ways to make a stake—if you got the right connections," retorted the Texan, gazing levelly into Pomeroy's eyes.

The sheriff's gaze sharpened. "Prospecting?" he queried.

"Wal," returned Craig with a faint smile, "you might call it that."

34

Pomeroy frowned, eyeing him closely. "Maybe, Craig, you should watch your step," he advised curtly.

"Sure will, Sheriff," the Texan assured him, straight-faced.

The lawman favored him with another searching glance, then turned abruptly away.

Craig stood eyeing the sheriff's broad back as he moved away. He saw Pomeroy check to bow to a woman toting a market basket, raise a jovial hand to a passing teamster, shout greetings to a townsman in a buggy. The hombre didn't pass up any bets when it came to cultivating the voters, he reflected. Well, he'd baited the hook and all he could do was stick around and hope for a strike. He couldn't go near Waxman now.

Noon was approaching. He dropped into the saloon, tossed his last quarter onto the mahogany in exchange for a bottle of beer, scooped up a fistful of pretzels from a bowl. The pretzels would stop his paunch from rattling, he considered, with no enthusiasm, but they made a heck of a midday meal.

He sat at the table by the window again, munching pretzels and watching shirt-sleeved townsmen saunter in, down their drinks and drift outside. No one seemed interested in a lone rider stretching out a beer by the window.

He had consumed the pretzels and was debating whether he had the gall to grab another handful on the strength of one drink when a rail-thin rider entered, bony featured, with a brooding bitterness in his eyes. The Texan tautened. This was the wiry outlaw who had blasted the Wells Fargo shotgun guard. A real hardcase, thought Craig, noting the tied-down holster as the newcomer moved to the bar.

The stranger ordered a drink, stood searching the saloon in the backbar mirror as he downed it. He poured another, dropped a coin on the mahogany and began winding between tables, packing his drink, heading for the Texan.

Scraping back a chair, he dropped down opposite Craig and set his glass on the table.

"Riding through?" he inquired without preamble, and his grating tone sounded as though it had been sifted through ashes.

The Texan lifted the makin's out of a pocket of his vest.

"Nope," he confessed. "I'm kinda sticking around, looking for an opening in my line."

The other sipped his drink, pale eyes probing like twin augers. "Jest what would your line be, mister?" he queried.

"I don't figure it's any of your business," said the Texan, his gaze meeting the other's.

"Mebbe not," agreed the bitter-eyed rider. "But I could steer a salty gent who packs a fast gun into a real bonanza."

"This brand of hombre?" inquired Craig. He yanked out the yellowed wanted dodger broadcasting Lester Collins' description, carefully smoothed its crackling folds and slid it across the table.

Unspeaking, the other looked it over. His head came up and his pale eyes weighed the Texan. Craig guessed he was mentally checking the description. "So you're on the dodge!" He pushed the dodger back.

"Maybe," admitted Craig with a faint smile. "Maybe I'm a bounty hunter on Collins' trail. Look me over, pard. Would anyone claim that an honest, hard-working hombre like me was that no-good, bank-busting Lester Collins, last lamped in Texas?"

"So thet's how you came to be packing all that gold on the westbound stage," murmured the other. His thin features creased into a parody of a grin. "You crave to get back into business?"

Craig shrugged. "I'm flat broke."

"Not any more," retorted the other. He fished out a fat roll, peeled off a twenty-dollar bill and pushed it across the liquid-stained tabletop. "You're hired, Collins! My moniker's Frosty Freeman."

"Punching cows?" The Texan grinned and picked up the bill.

Amusement gleamed in the outlaw's cold eyes. "Herding stock," he corrected, swallowed his drink and pushed back his chair. "Meet you here, sundown, and we'll get down to cases."

"It'll be a pleasure," drawled Craig, conscious of a surge of exhilaration. His gamble had paid off, quicker than he'd dared to dream. It was plain that Pomeroy had passed word to Freeman that a likely new recruit was in town, and the outlaw had promptly nosed him out.

He eyed the twenty-dollar bill that Freeman had pushed across the table, stuffed it into a pants pocket and rose. This called for a celebration—a thick steak and all the trimmings.

VIII

SHADOWS slid across the sage as two riders jogged eastward. Gradually, the nature of the terrain changed; the plain swelled into rolling foothills, girded with cowpaths. Craig guessed they must have reached the fringe of the Mesquito Hills. The Texan's elation at his success in penetrating the gang was tinged with disappointment, due to his failure to contact and warn Waxman. Through the afternoon he'd hung around town, hoping to meet the Pinkerton on the street so it would appear accidental. He could only guess that the sheriff would have someone watching Waxman. Well, he consoled himself, he'd find an excuse to ride back to town when they'd cleaned up whatever job Freeman had in mind, and nobody'd be watching *him*.

Darkness had thickened when Freeman, pulling ahead, wheeled through a jagged break in a squat butte's flank. Tailing the outlaw, Craig found himself riding between the eroding walls of a narrow canyon, looking up between rugged cliff tops that almost came together overhead. Through the gloom, he glimpsed the dull red glow of a camp fire, and the shadowy forms of two riders hunkered beside it. Beyond, their ponies were blobbed amid a thin screen of chaparral.

A big iron pot hung from a tripod over the spluttering greasewood and a sooted coffeepot sat steaming on the fringe of the fire. A wreck pan held tin cups and plates. At the base of a canyon wall bedrolls were heaped.

Freeman rode past the fire. Tailing him, Craig met the expressionless gaze of the burly outlaw he knew as Jake and the uneasy eyes of Brazos.

In the brush, Freeman piled stiffly out of leather and slackened cinches. The Texan followed suit.

When the new arrivals approached the fire, Brazos lifted off the pot with a forked stick and set it on the ground. "Dig in!" he invited, broke a hard chunk of frying pan bread onto a tin plate and indicated the viands with a callused hand.

His pards grabbed a cup apiece and dipped into the stew pot. One cup remained in the pan. Craig picked it up.

"Wyoming's," volunteered Freeman and reached for a chunk of bread. He jerked his head in the direction of the bedrolls. "Yuh can take over his soogans and Winchester, too. He sure won't be needing 'em no more." Wyoming, Craig guessed, must have been the recipient of the Wells Fargo guard's buckshot.

No further word was spoken as the four squatted around the fire, slurping stew. Now and again, Craig noted, the two he had roughed up in the saloon slid questioning glances in his direction.

They swilled out their tin cups in a bucket of water, passed the coffeepot around and began building smokes.

"Meet Lester Collins!" Freeman's harsh tones broke a long silence. "The hombre's dodging a Texas warrant f'r heisting banks." He chuckled dryly. "Stages should be a cinch."

"Call me Craig," put in the Texan.

"Wal, Craig, the big elephant is Jake and the runt's Brazos."

"I already met the gents," returned Craig with a faint smile. Jake grunted, scowling into his coffee. Brazos fingered his throat. "You figure I ain't forgot?" he demanded truculantly.

"You plan to do something about it?" prodded Craig.

Brazos stiffened, glaring across the flames. "Mebbe!" he snarled.

"Any time!" mocked the Texan.

"Simmer down!" barked Freeman. "There's no call to go on the prod. Craig's in. Let bygones be bygones."

"Hunky-dory!" growled Brazos, and suddenly grinned. "Wal, I already laid my barrel across his conk."

Craig ignored the gibe and eyed Frosty. "What's the deal?" he wanted to know.

Freeman tossed the dregs of his coffee aside, pitched

the cup into the wreck pan. "We divvy up half the take—five ways. Two shares to me, you boys get one apiece."

"Half the take!" echoed the Texan, raising his brows. "Who else cuts in?"

"How long you figure we'd stay in business bucking the law?" bit back the bitter-eyed bandit.

Craig raised his shoulders.

"And get this," continued Freeman, eyeing Jake. "From now on, outside the Express box, all we grab is dinero. No watches, no rings, no nothing. Jest greenbacks and gold."

That ruby ring had taught Pomeroy a lesson, thought Craig. Idly, he inquired, "When do we get busy?"

"Sunup!" Freeman threw back.

"The usual job?"

"A special job!" snapped the bandit. Craig wondered at the virulence in his tone.

The fire burned lower, guttering into glowing embers. Jake heaved to his feet, plodded toward the bedrolls. Brazos followed. Craig tossed a butt into the dying embers, rose too.

"Hold it!" barked Freeman.

The Texan paused, eyeing the bitter-eyed bandit with quick inquiry.

"Quit prodding the boys," rasped the renegade. "We don't stick together, we'll sure hang apart."

Craig smiled. "Sure, Frosty, sure!" he soothed.

Lying in a dead man's soogans, he watched the remnants of the fire graying into ashes. Well, reflected the Texan, he'd achieved his object. Now he was in solid with the stagecoach bandits. But what had it bought him? Likely Frosty Freeman had another holdup planned for the coming day. He had no option but to take part, which meant that forever he'd be tarred with the same brush as these curly wolves. If the stage company sprang a surprise, maybe loaded a coach with armed guards, he was likely to stop lead. Captured, he'd be hanged out of hand. Who'd ever swallow a story that he'd thrown in with the renegades to wreck their organization and recover his own stake? The idea of armed robbery stuck in his craw, too, and was hard to swallow. He'd always ridden on the right side of the law. Now he was aligned with the coyotes, and the taste was bitter.

A slim chance still offered to pull back, he pondered. With luck, he could make a getaway before dawn. Then he'd be no further ahead than when he'd been nursing a sore head and empty pockets in Wicker's Ford. The sheriff was crooked, and who else would listen to the accusations of a stranger—and a saddlebum at that? Nope, the musing Texan decided, he'd set his hand to the plow and now he had to follow the furrow to the bitter end. He rolled over and sank into sleep.

The feel of a sharp-toed riding boot prodding his ribs stirred Craig back to wakefulness. Yawning, he threw the soogans aside and fumbled for his boots. Cold gray light filtered into the canyon, and Freeman was striding away.

Buckling on his gunbelt, Craig came to his feet. The chill of dawn seemed to bite into the very marrow of his bones. Nothing remained of the fire but ashes, and no one seemed inclined to build another. Jake was awkwardly spooling his roll, while Brazos stood glumly twirling the cylinder of his .45, checking the loads. Freeman fished a bottle of bourbon, three-parts full, out of a gunnysack. He took a long pull, passed it to Jake. When it got around to Craig, the fiery liquor bit into his throat like a branding iron and set him choking. By the time he'd rolled up the canvas tarp and dirty blanket that served as bed, the others were rigging their mounts. He joined them, spread a blanket over the dun, swung the saddle into place. Someone had slipped a Winchester into the boot. The stench of whiskey mingled with the raw odor of horse droppings, and pungent oaths prickled the tainted air, as the outlaws, unshaven, frowsy, edgy, cursed fiddle-footing ponies.

Freeman stepped into leather, glanced around and growled, "All set?"

"I need .44 shells," threw back Craig, nodding at the Winchester.

"The magazine's full—fifteen loads," rasped the renegade, and raised his reins.

In a string, the four riders headed down the canyon.

Saddle leather creaking, the four jogged northward, through a chaos of tortured rock, wrapped in taciturn silence.

After a while, the warming sun seemed to melt the chill that lay on the spirits of the renegades. Brazos pulled up beside Jake and the two began trading disjointed talk. Frosty dropped back to Craig's stirrup. "You take the leaders," he grated. "And keep your trigger finger greased if you don't crave to be buzzard bait," he added.

The sun was high when Frosty led them into a gully, then a short arroyo that knifed through a tangle of barren hills patched with scrubby greasewood. Frosty acted, thought Craig, as though he'd been there before. A clump of mesquite was patched against the gray aridity of the arroyo. The bandit pulled rein behind it and dismounted.

The four tied their ponies. Freeman legged up the arroyo, the others dogging him. With no talk, the bandits busied themselves rolling boulders until a crude barricade blocked the cut. This done, Brazos plugged across to the further side and ducked out of sight in a clutter of rock. Jake lumbered toward a misshapen chunk of talus and awkwardly stretched out on his belly behind it. Frosty motioned to Craig and nodded at the barricade. The Texan took up position by the rough rock wall and lay watching the bitter-eyed bandit scramble up the eroding side of the gully. Split and seamed with crevices, the rock offered easy climbing. Frosty wriggled onto a bench about ten feet from the ground, began scraping together debris that littered the bench into a pile, screening his prone form.

Sweat lay cold upon the Texan's back as he lay prone, although scorching heat rays bit through his flannel shirt. He yanked off his Stetson and smeared beaded moisture from its sweatband. What in thunder was he rattled about? he asked himself irritably. This holdup was a pushover, no more than a chore to the three hardcases bellied down around the cut. Frosty might be a two-legged scorpion, but he had savvy. He'd picked his spot well, just beyond a sharp curve in the rough mountain road that angled through the gully. The stage driver wouldn't sight that barricade until he was on top of it. Boxed in by rocky walls, he couldn't swing the stage around. He would be trapped.

Realization then came to Craig that it wasn't the danger but the nature of the job that sickened his stomach. He was sure never cut out to be a road agent, he thought humorlessly. Right then, he would have cheerfully forfeited his lost stake to have been out of there.

Every nerve tautened as the faint yelp of a stage driver, muted by distance, reached his ears.

Frosty's dry tones grated from the ledge: "Cover that map, knothead!"

Hastily, Craig yanked his bandanna up over his nose, heard a click as Frosty levered a shell into the breech of his Winchester. The steady clip-clop of shod hooves on rock, the grinding rumble of iron-rimmed wheels, were plain now.

IX

THE SIX-HORSE TEAM swirled around the curve, stretched out in full gallop on the downgrade, a yellow Concord swaying and bouncing behind. Too late, the driver glimpsed the rock barricade, frantically hauled on the lines and jammed on the foot brake. The team piled up against the obstacle in a tangle of harness and threshing hooves; the cursing driver fought his milling team.

Craig, on his feet now, six-gun in hand, eyed the dust-shrouded melee. Frosty's yell, punctuated by a rifle shot, cut through the crunch of restless hooves. "All out—and no shenanigans!"

He slid down the wall, loose shale cascading after him, took up position to one side, Winchester slanted, alert and edgy as a questing lobo. Jake and Brazos approached the stage from opposite sides, guns out.

A melancholy file of passengers began spilling from the coach: a gaunt drummer, throwing affrighted glances around; two frozen-faced gamblers in frock coats; a gray-moustached cowman; a faded, middle-aged blonde wearing a stylish serge traveling dress and clutching a big, bone-handled purse with both hands; and last—Craig almost gasped with a quick intake of breath—Tom Waxman's solid form.

He saw the Pinkerton man take up position at the end of the file lined against the coach, and stand impassively looking the renegades over. Before his probing gaze reached Craig, the Texan moved so that the head and neck of a lead horse hid him from view. Jake, felt hat in hand, began to work down the row. Wallets, purses, greenbacks tumbled into the battered headpiece. It was a cut-and-dried operation, considered Craig, by now a monotonous chore to these hardcases. How come Frosty had claimed this heist was special? There wasn't even a Wells Fargo box.

Jake's big form slouched in front of the woman, who hugged the big purse against the swell of her breasts, mute indignation sparking in her affrighted eyes. Jake hesitated, threw an appealing glance over a shoulder in Frosty's direction.

"Pass!" rasped the renegade and Craig unconsciously released a sigh of relief when Jake shuffled on. Without further incident, he reached the end of the line.

"All in!" yelled Brazos. The passengers began hastily scrambling inside. Craig relaxed, glad it was over, dropped his gun into leather. A shot whipcracked through the air. With startled surprise, Craig whipped out the .45, thumbed the hammer and half-crouched, eyes searching. Frosty was lowering the Winchester from a shoulder, levering another shell into the breech. In a panic, passengers were crowding the stage door. Sprawled on the ground was Waxman's solid form, the shiny broadcloth suit dust-grayed, blood bubbling on his parted lips.

Brazos came up at a run and began to roll boulders aside. Fighting bewilderment, Craig gave him a hand.

Frosty motioned to the driver to pull ahead. The long lash of the whip crackled. Jouncing on its leather springs, the heavy Concord lurched forward as the horses put their weight on the traces. Quickly picking up speed, the vehicle whirled away, vanished behind a curtain of dust. Only the Pinkerton detective's body remained, bulging on the rocky trail.

With the other renegades, Craig legged toward the

corpse. "Why in thunder did you beef the hombre?" he demanded of Frosty, striving to keep his voice steady. Brazos and Jake, he saw, were as perplexed as he was.

"For damned good reason." Frosty's tone was charged with venom. "The bustard was a Pinkerton dick, framing to swing us." He dropped on one knee beside the still form and began rummaging through the pockets of the broadcloth coat and blood-soaked vest, tossing out an envelope, a block of stinkers, several cigars. Finally, with a grunt of satisfaction, he held up a small silver badge upon which was engraved *Tom Waxman. Pinkerton #413.*

"Lamp that!" he snarled, spat on the badge and threw it aside. Frosty moved off, heading back to the arroyo, the others at his heels. Craig lingered, dabbed down and gathered up the badge and the envelope, stuffed both hastily into a pants pocket, then jingled after the others. Waxman, he considered grimly, had signed his own death warrant when he confided in Sheriff Pomeroy.

Mentally, Craig swore that he'd never quit now, not until he saw Freeman strangle on a noose.

Night was beginning to shroud the hills when the renegades' trailworn ponies jogged into the canyon. Craig, still sickened by remembrance of Waxman's bloodied form, stripped off saddle and bridle, watered the dun, then busied himself rubbing down its coat with a rolled gunnysack. The others he noted, had merely slacked cinches. Although he'd always been finicky with horses, his prime reason for currying the dun was that it afforded him a chance to be alone and to think. Waxman's death changed the whole picture. Now he could count on no backing from the Pinkertons. He had to go it alone, play the part of Lester Collins and hope for a lucky break that would enable him to expose Pomeroy and his hirelings.

When he got through the fire was burning and Brazos, who seemed to double as cook, was hashing up beans and potatoes. Frosty had spread a blanket and squatted, engrossed in dividing a small heap of shining gold, big silver dollars and crumpled greenbacks into stacks. Craig hunkered beside him.

"No treasure box!" he commented.

"We bagged something bigger than a box," growled the renegade and pushed a stack of notes and coin toward the Texan. "Ain't such-a-much, but it beats nursing cows. Come and collect, Jake, Brazos."

Supper beneath their belts, the four hunkered around the fire, chewing quirlies and staring into the licking flames.

"Could be we're due to lay off stages for a while," said Frosty. "The boss is figuring on a switch. That smelter at Quartz is shipping a wagonload of gold ingots regular. Grab jest one of them shipments and we'll wallow in velvet."

"And buck a passel of armed guards," put in Brazos with gloomy distaste.

"Four to a wagon," threw back Frosty derisively. "We throw in with Smoky Joe's bunch and tally eight guns. Hell, the chore's easier than snatching candy from a kid."

So Pomeroy had another gang operating, registered Craig. Aloud he queried, "You mean we hole up in this damned canyon like groundhogs, with dinero burning a hole in our pants pockets?"

"Hell, no!" Frosty assured him carelessly. "Hit for town and tank up all you crave—jest keep a plug in your talk box."

Rays of the rising sun awoke Craig. Brazos was coaxing the fire into life, while Jake, a cigarette stuck between thick lips, squatted close by, a scowl on his heavy, brutish features. There was no sign of Frosty.

Talk between the two outlaws chopped off when Craig sat up. "Frosty around?" he hailed.

"Nope!" threw back Brazos shortly and a hunch hit the Texan that the hatchet-faced renegade still nursed sour memories of the saloon fracas. Maybe Jake, too. Could be, considered Craig, that the pair, free of the restraint imposed by Frosty's acrid tongue and fast gun, were set to make trouble. Cornered in that canyon, he was a sitting duck, and killing came easy to these vultures. It would be smart to get out—fast.

Watching the pair from the corner of an eye, he pulled

on his boots, rose and moved casually toward the ponies, buckling on his gunbelt.

Wasting no time, he rigged the dun and stepped into leather. Gaze straight ahead, he walked the pony toward the fire, swung around abruptly as he passed, right hand latched onto the butt of his holstered gun—and surprised Brazos stealthily lifting his .45 out of leather.

"Any time!" he challenged, checking the dun and whipping his own gun into view. Brazos' jaw slackened with surprise. He stared speechlessly, then his fingers loosened on the gun butt and the weapon slowly slid back into leather. Jake hunkered unmoving, no expression on his broad features.

"Adiós, amigos!" mocked the Texan, and roweled. The dun leaped forward, its hooves scattering dust and pebbles as it pounded away between the stark walls. When he wheeled out of the canyon, Craig dropped his gun back into the holster with a deep breath of relief and reined the pony down to a trot. He had another problem now, he considered wryly—staying alive. Brazos'd backed away in the canyon, but sooner or later they were destined to match cutters, if Brazos didn't grab a chance first to cut him down from behind. As for Jake, Craig figured the burly renegade would back Brazos in a pinch, but odds were he'd think first of his own hide.

Jogging toward town, the Texan's thoughts reverted to the murdered Waxman. Likely, he considered, when news of the killing percolated back to Pinkerton headquarters they'd dispatch another operator to carry on the investigation. And likely the new man would invite the sheriff's co-operation as Waxman had—to meet the same fate. There must be some way to outsmart the double-crossing Pomeroy. He pulled out the envelope Frosty had thrown aside while searching for the badge, felt paper inside. Withdrawing a folded sheet, he straightened it out and eyed slanted feminine handwriting. Written at its head was *14 Woodside Gardens, Fort Worth, Texas.* And it was signed *Your loving wife, Martha.* Before he'd read more than a few sentences, he knew that Waxman had left two children, too. A widow and two orphans, he reflected bitterly, created by that stinking sidewinder Frosty.

X

THE HUDDLE of shacks and adobes that was Wicker's Ford lay torpid beneath a fiery sun when Craig rode in. The clapboard hotel seemed more dilapidated than ever and the flag atop the pole in front of the relay station drooped dispiritedly. *What a dump to live and die in,* thought the Texan.

He rode into the shanty barn behind the hotel, stepped down, and tended to the dun.

The precise Miss Wicker was busily scrubbing dirty linen on a washboard in the wooden kitchen sink when he stepped in through a rear door. "Well!" she exclaimed, pausing and swiping off perspiration that beaded her forehead with a soapy arm. "So you're back! Did you locate a job?"

He shrugged. "Easy as eating striped candy. Dropped in to settle for the dun and liquidate that board bill. What might the score be, ma'am?"

"Isn't this . . . a little sudden?" she countered doubtfully.

He ignored the question, pulled out a wad of greenbacks, began skinning them off and dropping them on the kitchen table. "Thirty, forty, fifty dollars," he tallied, checked, and eyed her inquiringly. "Wal, how much more?"

"Fifty dollars would be plenty."

"Then fifty it is!" He pushed the little stack of bills toward her.

"Is—is it clean?" Her tone was hesitant.

"You fancy your greenbacks laundered?" he asked with amusement.

"You know what I mean!" she threw back. "How could you possibly have earned fifty dollars and more in a few days?"

"Poker, maybe."

She wiped off her wet forearms with a towel, eyeing his amused features with a perplexed frown, then gathered up the notes and thrust them down behind the V of her blouse. "I'll make out a bill of sale for the pony," she said, "and get your ring."

Craig raised a restraining hand. "Freeze onto the ring, ma'am," he begged. "That was my maw's. I'd hate to lose it at the tables."

"Do you have to gamble?"

"Reckon I jest can't resist the urge," he assured her straight-faced. "Guess its in my blood, liquor and cards."

"You just don't look the type." She weighed him with steady gray eyes, and added, frowning, "I still don't feel easy about that money."

Craig guessed that every dollar Miss Wicker had ever made had come hard, and she sure had an inflexible conscience. "Forget it!" he advised, offhand. "You got a room for me?"

"A dozen rooms," she told him ruefully. "The place is empty." The Texan detected a tremor in her voice and was consious of an inexplicable urge to gather Miss Wicker in his arms and comfort her. Then, he thought whimsically, she'd likely grab a frying pan and crown him. It was plain she was fighting a losing battle to earn a livelihood in this decaying old barn of an hotel, and she was the type that would continue to battle, with sturdy independence, until it finally collapsed about her ears.

Next morning, Craig was up and shaving before the sun showed. He had to get back to Cushman, he considered; Frosty would expect him to stick around town and he didn't crave to arouse any suspicion in the acrid renegade's mind, particularly since he now had Brazos on his neck. On the stroke of six he sauntered into the dining room, dumped his saddlebags and dropped onto a bench beside the long table. Miss Wicker, trim and neat despite the early hour, set a platter of smoking flapjacks before him and poured coffee. "You leaving so soon?" she queried.

"Can't make any dinero setting around here," he retorted, spilling molasses over the flapjacks.

Her lips compressed as she stifled a quick retort and she tip-tapped back into the kitchen.

Craig cleaned up the stack of flapjacks, pushed back his chair with a sense of comfortable repletion, slung the saddle-bags across a shoulder and hit for the barn.

In a contented mood, he spread a blanket across the dun and swung the saddle into place. It was a relief to be shut of that stinking bunch of renegades, even for a day, he considered, and the presence of Miss Wicker sure gave a lift to his spirits.

He tightened cinches, straightened, turned at the sound of footsteps on the loose planks behind him, to face the girl and a broad-shouldered stranger in rider's garb with a scraggy moustache and a deputy badge pinned to his loose-hanging vest. A long-barreled Colt was leveled in his right hand. Miss Wicker clutched a yellowed wanted dodger and tears glistened in her eyes. Before he could speak, she burst out, "So that's your trade!" and thrust the dodger at him. One glance and he knew the faded sheet described one Lester Collins, wanted for bank robbery in Texas. Unconsciously, he fingered his hip pocket. It was empty.

"I found this in your room," she accused, her voice quivering with emotion. "It matches! Oh, why did you have to come here?" With that, she dropped the dodger and spun blindly away, heading out of the barn at a stumbling run, long skirt flapping about her legs.

"Reach!" directed the deputy curtly.

Mind in a turmoil, the Texan slowly raised his hands shoulder-high. Mentally, he cursed his carelessness. It was plain that the dodger had slipped out of his pants pocket and had lain unnoticed on the floor of his room—until Miss Wicker entered to change the sheets. It was hopeless to attempt an explanation, he thought dejectedly. They'd both dub him a liar in face of the damning evidence of the dodger. What was more, this deputy could be as crooked as the sheriff.

He stood stiff-muscled while the lawman reached with his left hand and slipped the buckle of his gunbelt. It dropped and lay in a half-circle around his feet, covering the telltale dodger. With the same hand, the deputy lifted a jingling pair of handcuffs from a back pocket and expertly clicked the 'cuffs on Craig's wrists. He scooped up the gunbelt, picked up the dodger, folded it carefully and stowed it in a pocket. "Now," he said, "we'll take a ride."

Stirrup to stirrup, the two jogged westward along the

stage road. No talk passed between them. The deputy slumped in his saddle, riding loose, eyes half-closed against the glare of the flats. Craig was in no mood for talk. Not that his arrest meant anything; in fact it was likely to strengthen his position with the gang. And he had no doubt that the sheriff would quickly ease him out of the tight. But he hated to lose the confidence of that gray-eyed girl.

It was mid-morning when their ponies' hooves stirred the dust of Cushman's main street. Life in the countyseat crawled at its usual sluggish pace; Craig held his manacled wrists low, thankful that no one gave two passing riders more than a cursory glance.

They wheeled to the rail outside the red-bricked courthouse and clumped up the stairs. Sheriff Pomeroy was busy with papers at his desk, and a peg-legged old-timer chased dust with a bristle broom, when the deputy steered his prisoner through the doorway.

At sound of their jingling spurs, Pomeroy slewed around in his swivel chair. His glance fell on Craig, dropped to the handcuffs, and the prisoner read startled surprise in the brassy-blue eyes. When he spoke, however, his deep voice was bland and untroubled. "Wal, Tom, who you got there?"

The deputy dug out the wanted dodger, spread it and handed it to the sheriff with a flourish. "Lester Collins," he reported. "Picked the lobo up at the hotel in town. Wanted in Texas for bank robbery." With satisfaction, he told of the dropped dodger, and concluded, "The jasper came in on a westbound stage last week, checked into the hotel with a damaged conk, claimed road agents had lifted $3,600 he was packing." He chuckled. "Seems the bustard swallowed a dose of his own medicine." His tone quickened. "Say, Sheriff, when do I latch onto that five hundred?"

"Just as soon as it comes through from Texas," Pomeroy assured him breezily. "That was nice work, Tom. You can take off the 'cuffs now."

Hands released, Craig stood rubbing his chafed wrists.

"Empty your pockets!" directed the sheriff briskly. The prisoner dropped a stock knife, the makin's, a few creased greenbacks and some silver on the desk.

"Pull off your boots!"

Craig sank onto a chair, yanked off his high-topped riding boots. Pomeroy carefully shook them out, then ran his hands over the prisoner. "Guess he's clean," he commented and hailed the peg-legged man. "Lock him up, Sam!"

Craig followed Sam when he stumped out, the deputy trailing behind. The trio descended a wooden stairway at the rear end of the corridor and the prisoner found himself in a cavernous cellar—the courthouse basement—into which faint light filtered through metal gratings, high up. Along one side of the basement, a row of steel cells had been built against a wall. In one, a drunk sprawled in his vomit.

A steel gate clanged behind Craig.

Left alone, he stood peering around in the dim light. The cell had no furnishings beyond a discolored mattress thrown on a low bench, and a metal bucket set in one corner. Heavy beams criss-crossed overhead and his nose wrinkled at the foul stench, a composite of human excretia and unwashed bodies. From the dark recesses of the basement came faint squeals and scamperings.

Craig stretched out on his mattress and pondered on his predicament. One thing was sure, he reflected: his arrest would force Pomeroy to show his hand—unless Pomeroy dumped him, figuring him a liability now that his assumed identity was known. And he had no comeback, no concrete proof that the sheriff was tied in with the renegades. Pomeroy could ship him back to Texas in irons and he had no hope of convincing anyone that he was not the fugitive bank robber until he faced the sheriff of Lennox County, Texas, who had issued the warrant. And could be even the Texas sheriff wasn't personally acquainted with Collins. If his luck held sour he was liable to end up serving a long prison term in Huntsville Penitentiary. Sweating, he came to his feet and began restlessly pacing the cell.

XI

HOURS DRAGGED, but there was no further sign of Pomeroy or the peg-legged jailor. What meager light filtered through the gratings died. Craig hunched on the low bench that served as bed and stared glumly into the gloom, the squealing of the rats and the stentorian snoring of the drunk in his ears. He quickened to attention at sound of the hollow thump of a wooden leg. Packing a stable lamp, the jailor crossed the uneven dirt floor toward his cell and announced, "Jonathan Barker, the mouthpiece, is up at the office, primed to bail you out." Selecting a key from a tinkling collection on a large metal ring, he threw the gate open.

Relief flooded the prisoner. So Pomeroy had come through!

He followed the peg-legged man up the stairway.

A waspy little man with sideburns and a rusty frock coat stood by the sheriff's desk, summoning all his tarnished dignity.

"So you're Lester Collins!" he frowned. "Well, Collins, I have here an order, signed by His Honor Judge Perkins, authorizing your release on bail."

"Who'd put up bail for me?" inquired the prisoner, with a side glance at the sheriff. Pomeroy, however, seemed to have other matters on his mind. He stood by the narrow window, peering out into the fading light, while the toe of one polished boot beat a nervous tattoo on the floor boards.

"Only a fool would question freedom, young man," admonished the lawyer, "temporary though that freedom may be. Let it suffice that the shackles of the law are loosened."

Craig nodded impatiently; he was in no mood to wrangle words. He took his gunbelt from the jailor, buckled it around his middle, stuffed an envelope containing his scant belongings into a pocket. Darting another glance at the abstracted sheriff, he hit for the doorway.

There was one chore to be handled pronto, he decided, as he dropped down the courthouse steps. Angling across street, he headed for the hotel. As he strode along, he became aware of a curious air of tension that seemed to have fastened upon the town. Lamplight, streaming through the windows of stores and saloons, revealed knots of men bunched under the wooden canopies, engaged in acrimonious discussion; two townsmen were baiting an angry deputy;

everywhere, men seemed to be scanning copies of *The Cushman Clarion*.

He entered the lobby of the hotel and told the man behind the desk, "I need to write a letter. You got the makin's?"

The clerk silently dug out a writing pad, envelope and pencil, pushed them across the counter. Craig brought out the letter that had been in Waxman's pocket, stood eyeing it, chewing the pencil. Finally he turned the sheet over, wrote on the back, *Waxman was murdered by renegades in the Mesquito Hills. Sheriff Pomeroy crossed him. Warn the Pinkertons to be 'leery of Pomeroy.* He signed it *Burt Craig.* Folding the sheet, he stuck it in the envelope and dropped Waxman's badge in with it. But when it came to addressing the envelope he was stuck. He guessed the Pinkerton outfit was located somewhere in the East. Even if he knew their address, he considered, the letter could be weeks in transit. On impulse, he wrote, *U.S. Marshal, Tucson, Arizona Territory*, and sealed the envelope.

"Gimme a stamp," he said to the clerk and tossed a silver dollar on the counter, "and get yourself a drink."

"With pleasure!" beamed the other. "Stranger in town?"

Craig nodded. "What in thunder's going on here?" he wanted to know, as he affixed the stamp.

The clerk chuckled. "Carl Steiner—biggest man in town—and the reformers are on the warpath again—threatening a cleanup."

"Cleanup of what?" Craig dropped the letter in a slotted box marked MAIL.

The clerk lifted meaty shoulders. "Graft, they call it. Steiner never did hit it off with Sheriff Pomeroy. It's just local politics! Jack Pomeroy's got a big following. Last election a bunch of these do-gooders raised a stink but they got nowhere." He turned away to register a guest.

So that was what was bothering Pomeroy, thought Craig, heading back to the street.

When he pushed through the batwings of the Old Fruit, the saloon was packed with yammering patrons. Elbowing to the bar, he ordered a beer, pulled back out of the crush and, from habit, made his way to his former table by the window. It was vacant and someone had left a copy of

The Cushman Clarion lying on its stained top. He dropped onto a chair and picked the paper up. Black headlines caught his eye:

CLEANUP THREATENED
Reform Group Challenges Alleged Spoilers

Then his eyes skipped to a boxed announcement in the next column:

$5,000 REWARD
will be paid for evidence leading to the breakup of criminal gangs operating in San Marcos County and the exposure of public officials believed to be affording said criminals protection.

Carl Steiner, Chairman
Cushman Cleanup Committee.

Craig whistled softly. This was hitting Pomeroy straight from the shoulder. Seemed the local citizens meant business, but just how far would this reform committee get?

He looked up as a shadow dropped over the table and Jake's ungainly form bulked beside him. "Howdy!" Craig said offhand, then nodded at the headlines and advised with a faint grin, "You better skeedaddle."

Jake spat. "Hell, we got them do-gooders thrown and hogtied. I been hunting over all creation f'r you, Craig. Frosty craves a word, urgent."

"Frosty?" Craig's glance swept the crowded saloon. "Where?"

"In the poker parlor—end of the bar."

The Texan scraped back his chair. "Hunky-dory," he said, then added, "You ditched Brazos?" It was the first time he had seen the two apart. Always, he reflected, they stuck together like two shoats in the same pigpen. His glance quickened at a momentary hesitation in the burly bandit's reply. "The runt's—sick," Jake mumbled. He was too slow a thinker to be a convincing liar, thought Craig. What was he covering up? Then the Texan tensed with surprise. Through the dusty window, beyond Jake, he caught a

54

glimpse of a wiry form, jingling past on the plankwalk. There was no mistaking those thin, harsh features. It was Frosty Freeman.

Craig thought fast. Just why was Jake toling him into the private room where big poker games were staged? The answer came in a flash—Brazos. Brazos was nursing that grudge and nothing but a payoff would satisfy him. Likely he was waiting in the darkened room, primed to blast Craig when the door opened and he was outlined by the lights of the saloon.

Craig eyed Jake levelly. "You plumb certain Frosty craves me in that room?"

"You naming me a liar?" blustered the burly renegade.

He could call Jake's hand right now, considered the Texan, but what would it buy him? He'd still have Brazos on his neck. If there had to be a showdown it might just as well be now.

Jake stood watching, a pleased grin slowly spreading over his broad features, as Craig began to shoulder a path across the crowded saloon.

When the Texan reached the closed door of the poker parlor, he paused, lifted his .45 out of leather, thumbed back the hammer. Mentally, he reviewed the layout of the room beyond.

With a quick motion, he threw the door open, ducked and hurled himself full length across the threshold. As he hit the floor—outstretched—a gun lanced scarlet and a slug whined over his head. By the flash he glimpsed the lower portion of a man, standing by the far wall. The poker table cut off the upper part of his body from view. His own gun flamed red. He heard the door slam behind him and black obscurity walled him in. Quickly, he rolled. Another report filled the small room with thunder and he choked back an urge to cough as powder fumes bit into his throat. Silence now engulfed the darkened room.

Sprawled out on the floor, eyes straining, ears acute, Craig tried to locate his would-be assassin.

Seconds dragged, weighted by tension, but still there was no further sound in the room beyond the muted drone of men's voices beyond the door. Nerves taut as fiddlestrings, the Texan moved carefully, slipping a cartridge from his gunbelt. Braced for quick action, he tossed the cartridge into the darkness on his left. It tinkled onto bare boards. A gun blazed with an abruptness that showed other nerves besides his own were edgy. Plain in the powder blast, he focused on Brazos' stocky form, crouched against the wall ahead. Once—twice—three times his Colt thundered and bucked, as he threw lead beneath the tabletop. Again, darkness shrouded the room, a darkness through which sound of the labored gasping of a man in mortal agony seeped to the Texan's ears. As he lay listening it grew fainter—finally died.

Wary of a trick, Craig began slowly worming across the floor in the direction from which the sound had issued, gun gripped in his fist. Blindly easing forward, he collided with a chair, froze as it rattled against another. No gunshot shattered the brooding quiet. More confident now, he writhed ahead. Groping, his fingers touched a boot. He lifted the outstretched leg. It dropped limply. Swiftly changing position he scratched a stinker into fire. The wavering light revealed Brazos' slack form, spraddled out. Wide open, his eyes were fixed in a lifeless stare. The fingers of one hand still loosely enfolded the ivory grips of a gun butt.

XII

THE DOOR burst open and yellow light flooded the room as a flood of excited men surged in, two deputies in their forefront. Craig came to his feet as the tide eddied around the body on the floor. A hard-eyed deputy grabbed his shirtfront, slammed him back against the wall and snatched his gun from the holster. "What's going on here?" the lawman wanted to know.

"A grudge fight," Craig told him.

The second deputy bent and loosed the ivory-butted gun from the dead man's stiffening fingers. He pressed the release key, dropped the cylinder into a palm, shook the cartridges out. "Three empties," he reported and sniffed the barrel. "Fired recent."

"You'll find five empties in mine," volunteered Craig. "Every slug loosed in self-defense."

"What'll we do with the trigger-happy rooster, Tod?" inquired the deputy whose beefy hand was still latched onto the Texan's shirt.

"Book the bustard!" returned the other deputy promptly. "Disturbing the peace."

Remembrance of the rat-infested, gloomy jail flashed into Craig's mind. No sooner out than in again, he considered drearily. Pomeroy would likely consider this shoot-out a personal vendetta and leave him to rot in that black hole beneath the courthouse.

The two deputies hustled him outside. Frosty and Jake were standing by the bar. Frosty's bleak scrutiny betrayed nothing, following as the lawmen steered him across the saloon floor, but Craig read glowering hatred in Jake's scowling gaze.

When the three clumped down the corridor of the courthouse and entered the sheriff's office, Pomeroy swung around to eye the prisoner.

"You again!" It was almost a snarl and Craig guessed the sheriff's nerves were on a raw edge. "Well, what's the charge?" demanded Pomeroy brittlely of the deputies.

"Disturbing the peace. Mixed it with another jasper in the Old Fruit and salivated the hombre," recited one, as tonelessly as though he were reporting a drunk.

"Strictly self-defense," put in the Texan. "Brazos laid for me, fired the first shot."

The sheriff's attention quickened and Craig guessed the name was familiar. "Any witnesses?" inquired Pomeroy sharply.

"Nope," said a deputy. "They shot it out in the dark, behind the closed door of the poker parlor."

The sheriff stood fingering his chin, eyeing the prisoner with moody indecision. Spur chains jingled. Frosty strode through the doorway, Jake slouching at his heels. The bitter-eyed bandit brushed past the deputies. Craig read relief in Pomeroy's eyes and guessed the sheriff had weightier matters than a saloon shooting on his mind.

"Sheriff," rasped the renegade. "I lamped the start of this

fracas. Some drunken saddlebum pushed the gent you got there into gunplay. He didn't have no choice but shoot."

"Clear case of self-defense," murmured Pomeroy. "Get back on the street," he told the deputies. "I'll handle this."

"How about my gun?" demanded Craig, as they moved toward the door.

The deputy who'd grabbed him lifted the .45 from beneath his waistband and slammed it on the desk, with a hard glance in the direction of the prisoner. Odds were, reflected Craig, he'd figured to peddle it.

Scarcely had the deputies' heavy steps died away down the corridor when Frosty picked up the gun and tossed it to Craig. "You two hairpins stick around outside," he directed, and added venomously, "Lock horns and I'll make it my personal business to let daylight into both your hides."

Craig followed Jake's lumbering form. The hulking bandit paused at the head of the steps, squatted beside the doorway. Craig dropped down on the further side. Techy as two strange dogs, they hunkered in silence. Craig made a smoke and wondered what was transpiring inside the office. Maybe, he mused, the sheriff was scared that one of his hirelings would be tempted by the reward to spill his guts to Steiner. The bunch lined up to harry the stages would sell out their own mothers if they thought they could get away with it. Pomeroy was skating on thin ice and it was liable to crack most any time.

Appearance of Frosty interrupted his cogitations. Trading no talk, the three mounted and rode out of town. Craig noted that Frosty, in the lead, headed east instead of west. So they were not returning to the canyon, he thought; something was afoot. He pulled up to the renegade's stirrup and inquired, "We hitting the gold shipment?"

"Yep!" snapped Frosty. "One heist and we pocket enough dinero to choke a mule. Then we hit for the border and lay doggo f'r awhile."

The Texan remembered Brazos' claim that four armed guards rode with each shipment. "Hit 'em with three guns?" he prodded.

"Seven guns," bit back Frosty. "We're throwing in with Smoky Joe's bunch."

So that was how the sheriff had decided to handle the situation, considered Craig. He'd steer the whole kit and caboodle across the border, where they'd be safe from exposure to five thousand dollar rewards. And the carrot designed to toll them south was the rich loot offered by a gold shipment. For a while, the stages would roll unmolested. Pomeroy would claim to have cleaned up the road agents and the reform group would run out of ammunition. Had to hand it to Pomeroy; he was slick. Trouble was that the unexpected move knocked Craig's plans into a cocked hat. Once across the border, the renegades would be out of reach of posses and Pinkerton agents. Seemed that prospects of recovering his own money faded every day. But he had more than the loss of a stake to spur him now. Payment was overdue for Waxman's murder. And that was not enough. Without the aid of a crooked sheriff none of this crime and killing would have been possible. Pomeroy had to be exposed as behind it all, and with evidence concrete enough to convince a jury and the voters of San Marcos County. All he could do was hang on and hope that, sooner or later, Lady Luck would deal aces.

The terrain over which the three were riding was strange to Craig, and he could see little of it in the starlight. After a while, the rolling swales began to break up and the ponies' hooves clattered on rock. Vague in the night, hills began to bulge around and ridges were sharply etched against the stars.

Abruptly, Frosty reined down into an arroyo, following a trail invisible in the darkness. The others tailed him, whipped by impeding branches. They broke into a cleared space. The fitful light of a camp fire, built against an eroding cutbank, played upon the harsh features of four riders squatting around it. This, Craig concluded, must be Smoky Joe's gang.

One of the riders straightened and sauntered toward them when they stepped out of leather. He was short, thickset, with a bull neck and square features crowned by a tangle of coarse black hair. A ragged growth of beard sprouted from his heavy jowls and his eyes were reddish, opaque, glittering in the firelight and restless as those of a questing cougar. This, decided Craig, must be Smoky.

Frosty gestured for Jake to take the saddle horses. The lumbering renegade scowled at the chore, but he gathered the dangling reins without protest and shambled down the arroyo. Somehow, Craig sensed, his downing of Brazos had raised him a step in Frosty's estimation.

The thick-set rider drifted up and stood, thumbs hooked in a sagging cartridge belt, looking Craig over. His probing gaze dropped to the lone star fashioned in white beads upon each boot top. "Texan," he mused. "How come you quit God's country?"

"Dodging a warrant," supplied Frosty. His thin features crinkled into a humorless grin. "And packing a mess of gold—which he kindly donated." He told of the stage holdup in the Mesquito Hills and the chunky outlaw roared with laughter. Then Smoky Joe's features straightened. "Don't lamp Brazos around," he said.

"The jasper's buzzard bait," returned Frosty shortly. "Crossed guns with Craig."

The camp was astir with the first flush of dawn. With the others, Craig washed down a mess of fried sowbelly and beans with scalding coffee. Smoky led the way out of the arroyo and west, six riders stringing behind him.

Smoky breasted a low ridge and checked his mount. The others crowded him, eyeing a wide, shallow valley outspread below and the tortuous course of a dry wash twisting across it. Beyond, seared-looking hills, pocked with dark canyons, marched in ragged ranks until, obscured by distance, they merged into the flanks of the mighty Copperheads, whose somber mass was raw-etched against the skyline.

Frosty uttered a sharp exclamation and leveled a bony finger, pointing up valley. Faint with distance, a dust streamer crawled toward them.

"The wagon, b'Gawd!" pronounced Smoky. "Le's ride!"

The ponies' hooves slipping and skidding on loose rock, the party began winding down the slopes. When they approached the valley floor, Craig saw that a well-defined trail traversed its length. Smoky lifted his pony to a canter, heading for the dry wash. His intent was plain to the Texan: to ambush the wagon packing a shipment of gold ingots where the trail crossed the wash.

The seven riders dropped down into the dry watercourse and began winding between high cutbanks along its twists and turns. At the crossing, the cavalcade halted. Here the banks on either side had been broken down and rudely graded. The sandy bed of the crossing was pocked by hooves and rutted by wagon wheels.

Amid a scurry of hooves and swirl of confusion, the renegades piled out of leather, slid Winchesters out of saddle boots and spread along the wash to take up positions. A bearded outlaw choused the horses out of sight beyond a bend and steel clinked on rock as men became busy digging toeholds in the cutbank with bowie and stock knives.

Hatless, peering up the valley through squat brush that fringed the wash, Craig watched the drifting dust plume steadily draw closer, stirred by a slow-moving wagon. At arm's reach on his right, Frosty was focusing a battered telescope. "I'll be doggoned!" he suddenly exclaimed. "There ain't but one driver and two outriders. This heist is a cinch."

"You plumb certain the wagon's packing ingots?"

"Sure as shooting," asserted the bitter-eyed bandit. "Smoky got word last night from a lookout in town."

As Frosty had said, this heist promised to be as easy as snatching candy from a kid, thought Craig, but somehow it didn't make good sense that a gold shipment would be left practically unguarded, not when it was common knowledge that San Marcos County was infested with road agents.

XIII

Boots planted in the niche he had hacked in the cutbank, Craig watched the dust cloud steadily roll closer and considered humorlessly that his trip to Arizona Territory had sure brought some surprises. A month back, he reflected, he would have labeled anyone plumb crazy if they'd suggested that he'd shortly be a member of a renegade gang bent on highjacking a gold shipment. Maybe he would have shown better sense if he'd beaten it back to Texas instead of nursing loco notions about salvaging that stake.

Now the wagon, flanked by two outriders, was plain to the eye, as it lumbered along behind a four-horse team, stirring a fog of lazy dust.

It was an open wagon, Craig noted, the driver slacked on a box seat clipped to the bed. Heavily laden, too. That was apparent from the sluggish roll of the body as the nodding team hauled it over the bumps and breaks of the uneven trail. If there'd been a top he would have suspected that the canvas concealed a passel of armed guards. But it was plain that the gold's only escort were the two riders, one drifting on either side, well out to avoid the ever-rising dust. Sitting ducks for seven armed men, he thought. That smelter was mighty careless of its gold.

Not a hundred paces distant now, he could see the teamster's swarthy features as the man slouched on the box, the brim of a shapeless felt hat yanked down over his eyes. Suddenly the man he was watching straightened with a startled yell, jerked the team to a halt. Likely, thought Craig, he'd glimpsed the reflection of sunlight on the steel barrel of a leveled Winchester. Well, no power on Earth could save that gold shipment now.

As the team rattled to a stop, hidden guns along the wash spewed flame and thunder. The driver tumbled off the box, arms and legs whipping, while the team tangled in threshing, snorting disorder. The lash of gunfire promptly blasted one outrider out of the saddle. His terrorized pony, stirrups dancing, streaked off. On the further side of the wagon, the second rider whirled his mount, flattened across the pony's withers and roweled frantically. The merciless guns, concentrated now, scourged horse and rider with hot lead. The pony turned a complete somersault, impelled by the impetus of its wild gallop, crashed down. Its rider arced through the air, hit the ground with a flat thud and lay unmoving.

The mingling roar of gunfire died as quickly as it had erupted. Exultant shouts tearing from their throats, renegades began scrambling out of the wash, running clumsily toward the wagon, which was now jolting convulsively around, jerked by the panic-stricken team. Two renegades fastened onto the heads of the plunging leaders, striving to quiet them, while the rest bunched around the wagon like bees around honey—or wolves around a kill. Smoky set a boot on a spoke, hauled up into the bed and began peeling off a heavy tarp that covered the load. A triumphant yell left the throats of the renegades clustered around as four great slugs, gleaming dull yellow, were revealed. Smoky checked the outcry with a savage gesture, stood scowling down at the booty.

Craig, peering over the edge of the box, grasped what irked the thick-set renegade. Gold was commonly cast into brick-size ingots, about twenty-seven pounds in weight, easily transported and handled. But the four huge slugs lying in the wagon must have scaled at least two hundred and fifty pounds apiece, too cumbersome to be manhandled or packed on ponies. There was no possible way to carry them off, except in the wagon. The outfit that freighted the gold, he reflected, had outsmarted them. This shipment was practically bandit-proof. A fortune in gold was in the renegades' grasp but they couldn't move the massive slugs. He almost laughed out loud.

Baffled silence cloaked the raiders as realization of their predicament sank in. Cursing, Smoky thrust back his Stetson, and stood raking a tangle of hair with the fingers of one hand. "Guess we gotta cut them chunks up," he decided.

"Yeah!" drawled Frosty. "With what?"

Ignoring the caustic interruption, the stocky renegade continued, "First we run this wagon into the hills. Then we cache the slugs and get us some hacksaws."

"You figure we got time?"

"We got nothing but time," retorted Smoky.

Frosty raised his thin shoulders and turned away, disgust mirrored on his thin features. Abruptly, he swung back.

"Nothing but time!" he mocked. "Take a gander over there."

All heads swiveled. Dust was again smoking across the gray, rock-etched expanse—dust churned up by a compact body of horsemen sweeping down the trail at a fast canter. Craig figured there were a dozen or more. As neat a trap as had ever been sprung, he thought. While the wagon moved ahead, under light guard, its real escort followed, out of sight but within hearing of a rifleshot. When the lash of gunfire awoke the echoes, they'd plunged home the steel and were now hurtling into action.

"Git back to the wash!" yelled Smoky, and set the example. He jumped out of the wagon, his bowed legs pumping frantically as he plunged for cover. In a panic, the others joined him, the gold forgotten, racing for the dry watercourse.

Breathing hard, Craig slid over the brink of the wash, felt the impact in every joint as he dropped amid a shower of grit and hit the bed, hastily scrambled up the bank to eye their pursuers. Rattled, some of the renegades were already throwing useless lead.

Without a pause in their pace, the bunch of riders split, half angling for one end of the wash, and the remainder hurtling for the other. Realization came to Craig that the outlaws, outnumbered two to one and about to be outflanked, were doomed. And it was quickly plain that others nursed the same idea. The scuffle of boots behind him and the sound of men's hard breathing pulled his head around. In blind panic, men were racing along the wash, heading for their ponies. Without hesitation, he dropped and joined the retreat.

Stumbling over broken rock, jostled by gasping men, all well aware that capture meant a strangulation jig, he rounded the bend beyond which the ponies were bunched—and jerked to an abrupt stop. Opaque eyes glittering, Smoky crouched in front of the ponies, six-gun leveled, holding back his panting, terrified followers with the threat of the forty-five.

"We ain't dumping that gold," he gritted. "You bustards fight, or swallow lead." Craig saw Frosty slide behind Jake's burly form and jerk his own iron. It spat red death. Smoky teetered, dropped. Before he hit the ground, a rush of men charged over him. The wash was transformed into a maelstrom of cursing men, plunging horses, choking dust.

64

Mounted men began to cut out of the melee, all possessed of one urge—to get out of range of the pursuing horsemen's guns.

Struggling amid the turmoil of men and horses, Craig found his dun and hauled into leather. Urging his mount up the slope where the banks had been leveled to make a wagon crossing, he broke into the open and began racing down the valley. Ahead of him, renegades were madly spurring in all directions, each animated by his own idea as to where escape lay. Craig swung around in the saddle, surveying his back trail. Their assailants were still down in the wash, hidden from view. Fifty paces or so behind him, Jake pounded along. Always slow-moving, he'd been last to get away.

Lead droned. A slug glanced off a nearby rock in whining ricochet. He sensed a break in the rhythm of the dun's smooth action. A tremor passed over its body. It crashed down. Craig balled as he spilled from the saddle, rolled and weaved to his feet. Jake streaked past and he threw up a hand in an appeal for help. But the burly outlaw, eyes fixed ahead, thundered past. "You lousy bustard!" called the Texan. The big roan Jake straddled could easily have carried both of them out of danger. Other fleeing renegades were now no more than dots, dabbing in and out of view as they threaded through broken terrain.

Three horsemen emerged from the wash. Like questing hounds, they swooped toward him. The butt of Craig's Winchester protruded from its boot, the weapon jammed beneath the dead pony's shoulder. He jumped for it, wrenched the rifle clear, dropped down behind the swelling barrel of the dun, attempted to lever a cartridge into the breech. The action jammed. Throwing the useless weapon aside, he snatched his .45 out of leather.

His three assailants whirled around him, beyond effective range of the Colt, like Comanches on the plains. One curbed his mount, swung out of leather and bellied down, Winchester in hand. His two pards circled to right and left, followed suit. Helpless, pinned down from three sides, the Texan hugged the ground. The three could now cut him to, pieces at leisure, he considered, with bitter resignation. He had no more chance than a rabbit in a wolf's jaws.

XIV

CRAIG tossed out his gun, jumped up, hands stretched high, and stood braced for the impact of hot lead.

A husky rider with a ropy yellow moustache rose off the ground and began cautiously easing toward him, rifle slanted. "Git a rope!" he yelled to one of the others.

They brought up their horses, lashed the prisoner's hands behind him and stood looking him over, building smokes.

"What'll we do with the lobo, Jesse?" inquired one, a wizened rider, with lumpish cheekbones.

The yellow-moustached man shrugged. "Guess that's up to Tiny." He sauntered to his mount, loosed a coiled rope, carelessly made a loop, dropped it over Craig's head and jerked it tight.

"Let's go!" he said. In a knot, the three began jogging back toward the wagon. At the lead rider's stirrup, the prisoner trotted to keep pace, like a dog on a choke collar.

Padding through the dust, he saw that men were packing the forms of the slain outriders toward the wagon, around which the rest of the guard was bunched. When the trio rode up, men crowded around, looking the prisoner over with hard eyes. Craig returned their scrutiny with tight-lipped indifference. He figured that his string had run out and nothing he could say would help any.

A bull of a man, leathery-featured, pushed carelessly through the ring of onlookers, checked in front of the prisoner and stood sizing him up.

"So you corraled one of the lobos!" he commented, obviously in charge.

"What'll we do with him, Tiny?" inquired the rider with lumpy jaws.

"String the bustard up!" yelled someone, and there was a growled chorus of approval.

The big man grinned. "Nope, boys, not today. You know McCloud's a stickler for the law. This jasper will hang, but he'll hang regular. Guess we'll just head him for town."

Ignoring mutterings of dissent, he turned to the yellow-moustached rider. "Set the hombre on that buckskin we found in the wash, Jesse," he directed. "You and Baker run him back to Quartz, and take word that we're going ahead with the wagon to Tucson." He chuckled. "And tell Mc-Cloud that my idea for casting two hundred and fifty pound ingots worked like a charm." He raised his voice. "Wal, let's ride!"

The prisoner relaxed with unspoken relief. Seemed he had another lease on life. The big boss, this McCloud hombre, was a stickler for the law, Tiny had said. Which meant that he would be handed over to the sheriff—and the sheriff was Pomeroy. Seemed the man he detested might ace him out of a date with St. Peter.

They set him on the buckskin Smoky Joe had once forked, slipped off the noose and lashed his wrists to the horn. The rider called Jesse took the buckskin on the lead and the other guard brought up the rear.

Leaving the valley behind, the three beat through broken country that grew progressively wilder as the sun moved higher. Craig's wrists were raw from the rope and his throat was cindery-dry when they finally rounded the shoulder of a hill and began dropping down a twisting wagon road. They traversed a long gulch lined with drab constructions of rock or brick, and they reined up in front of a square-built building. Jesse dismounted, loosed the rope that secured the prisoner's wrist to the horn. "Git down!" he ordered.

When Craig slid stiffly to the ground, his captor yanked his arms behind his back and pinioned him again.

"Hell!" protested Craig. "I ain't a hog!"

"In my book you're a doggoned rattlesnake," threw back the other, and thrust him in the direction of the brick building.

On a plate affixed to the front door, the words, QUARTZ MINING AND DEVELOPMENT CO. JOHN MCCLOUD, SUPERINTENDENT, were lettered.

They passed through the doorway and Craig was hustled across a drab office into a back room.

At their entry, the man he judged to be John McCloud

swung away from a rolltop desk and sat scrutinizing him with cold blue eyes. For several moments the man at the desk focused on the prisoner's trail-stained, dust-plastered form, then he inquired in crisp, precise accents, "Just who might this be, Jesse?"

"A murdering polecat, Mr. McCloud." Jesse eyed his prisoner with disgust, then told of the holdup. Finally, he delivered Tiny's message, and concluded, "The boys woulda swung the bustard, but Tiny said to bring him in."

"And showed good sense!" approved the mine superintendent. "Lynch law is a reversion to barbarism. The veriest scoundrel is entitled to due process of law." He continued to eye the prisoner's unshaven, grimy features, a faint frown knitting his forehead.

"Do you admit that you were involved in this highjacking attempt?" asked the superintendent.

The prisoner raised his shoulders resignedly. Why waste words, he reflected. To McCloud—or any other man—his explanation would seem fantastic. And, since he was due to be handed over to Sheriff Pomeroy, that explanation would be a ticket to boothill—Pomeroy would make sure that he never left that stinking hole under the courthouse alive.

"Well?" prompted the superintendent, his tone edged.

The prisoner stood with locked lips.

"You leave me no choice but to hand you over to the law," said McCloud shortly. With a thin smile, he added, "The wages of sin, you know."

The wages of sin in San Marcos County, thought the prisoner, with faint derision, were a fat roll and high living. Pomeroy would spring him faster than hell could scorch a feather. It seemed that Lady Luck was smiling again.

"Take him away, Jesse, and guard him closely," directed the superintendent. "I'll send word to Sheriff Kirby to pick him up."

"Kirby!" exclaimed the prisoner. "The sheriff's Jack Pomeroy!"

"Not in Mineral County," returned McCloud shortly. "You'll find that we give criminals short shrift. We do not share San Marcos County's somewhat unsavory reputation for law enforcement."

Craig felt as though he had been slugged with an eight-pound sledge. The thought that the gang had ridden out of San Marcos County to highjack the gold shipment had never entered his mind. Numb from shock, he found the yellow-moustached man steering him toward a squat, windowless rock hut which looked like a disused powder shack, high on the hillside. Its heavy-timbered door sagged open. Prodded by his guard, Craig toiled up the slope and stumbled into darkness when the door slammed behind him. Arms still lashed, he edged forward in the gloom, collided with a rough wall. Drearily, he sank down. That mine superintendent had sure trumped his ace, he considered with wan humor. If he escaped the rope, he'd probably spend the rest of his days plaiting hair bridles. He'd sure left his luck behind in Texas.

XV

THE LOCKUP at Mineral King, countyseat, was a cut above the gloomy hole in which Craig had been briefly incarcerated in Quartz, but it stank like any other jail.

A passage ran down its length, giving admittance to a row of six thick-walled cells. Craig's cell was cool and quiet —too quiet. The ponderous adobe walls blocked out all sound and he saw no one, not even the jailor who thrust his meals through a trap in the ironbound door.

Days dragged by, the monotony of weary hours unbroken. At times Craig restlessly prowled the packed earth of the small square of floor; at others, he flopped on the bench that served as bed, staring hopelessly at the square vigas that supported the roof overhead. Trouble was, he couldn't summon up a flicker of hope. To the world, he was an outlaw, caught red-handed. Nothing lay ahead but a noose or living death.

The badge of a U.S. deputy marshal was pinned to Brick Harper's gray shirt, although no one ever looked less like a lawman. Harper was lanky, loose-jointed, with a built-in grin and a wide, humorous mouth. His eyes held the bland innocence of a day-old calf, but they veiled a shrewd mind, not to speak of unlimited gall.

Forking a leggy buckskin, the deputy dropped down the grade into Quartz and swung his loose-jointed form out of leather outside the brick building that housed the offices of the Quartz Mining & Development Co.

In response to his drawled inquiry, a clerk indicated the superintendent's closed door. Ignoring the formality of knuckling the door, Harper turned the handle and strolled inside.

At sound of the opening door, Superintendent McCloud swung around in his swivel chair, brittle protest in his cold eyes.

With a cheerful nod, the visitor hooked up a straight-back chair, spread his long form over it and stretched out long legs. "Harper, Deputy United States Marshal, Tucson," he announced offhand, and jerked the makin's out of a pocket of his dangling horsehide vest.

"Well, what can I do for you?" inquired McCloud with frigid politeness.

"Just give me a little information," drawled Harper. "Where'd you stash that outlaw your boys brought in?"

"I handed the man over to the county sheriff, as required by law," replied McCloud stiffly. "He will remain in custody until the circuit judge holds court, when I shall file the requisite charges. Frankly, I don't think the case comes within the jurisdiction of the federal authorities."

"Maybe you're right, maybe not," returned the visitor equably. "Right now, Uncle Sam's bothered by stage stick-ups in San Marcos County—stages packing U.S. mail. Guess that comes within our jurisdiction."

"This man was one of a gang that attempted to high-jack a gold shipment."

Harper smiled benignly. "Yep, Tiny wised me up. Tiny brought in four stiffs, three of your boys and Smoky Joe. Smoky served a term in Yuma—armed robbery. His stamping ground of late has been San Marcos County."

"So?"

70

"I kinda figured there might be a tie-in with the stage holdups."

"Extremely unlikely, in my opinion," said the superintendent brusquely.

"This hombre the sheriff's holding—you acquainted with his moniker?"

"He claims it's Craig, Burt Craig, a Texan."

The deputy whistled softly. "Can you beat that?" he murmured. "Could be I hit the jackpot." He fished in a pants pocket, brought out a creased sheet, smoothed it out and handed it to McCloud. Aloud, the superintendent read:

"Waxman was murdered by renegades in the Mesquito Hills. Sheriff Pomeroy crossed him. Warn the Pinkertons to be leery of Pomeroy—Burt Craig."

Frowning, McCloud looked up. "Just what does this mean?"

"Waxman was a Pinkerton dick, hired by the Butterfield Stage Company to look into these holdups." A tightness had crept into the deputy's easy tones. "There's a payoff due." He drew on his smoke, then continued, "I'd say this Craig was involved. That letter came out of Waxman's pocket and his badge was dropped in with it."

"Certainly he was involved," retorted McCloud with a wintry smile. "He's simply trying to muddy the trail and blacken Pomeroy's name."

Harper reached and casually retrieved the letter. "So you figure it that way?"

"It's obvious!" asserted the superintendent. "The fact that Craig robbed Waxman of his badge and a letter proves he was one of the murderers. Mailing both to you is plainly a slick trick to discredit Sheriff Pomeroy. Haven't criminals always been arch enemies of lawmen?"

"Could be," murmured the deputy. "Anyways, it's the first break we've had. Kinda feel I should brace this Craig."

"He'll probably have a smooth story to save his neck," said McCloud dryly. "They built Yuma Penitentiary for men of his stripe."

"There's a lot in what you say, Mr. McCloud," admitted Harper with a bland smile. He straightened lazily. "Guess I'll mosey along."

The superintendent nodded shortly and watched his lanky visitor drift out of the office. It was not surprising that crime flourished, he reflected irately, when enforcement of the law was entrusted to such types. That gullible nonentity would be better employed nursing cows than matching his wits against lobos of Craig's type.

The prisoner was sprawled on his bench, numbly staring at the ceiling, when the hinges of the heavy wooden door grated and it rasped open. Craig sat up when a lanky rider sauntered in, carelessly hunkered against the far wall. A deputy U.S. marshal's badge glinted on his shirt front.

The visitor busied himself making a smoke, tossed sack and papers to the prisoner. Craig eagerly fashioned a cigarette; he hadn't enjoyed a smoke for so long he'd most forgotten when.

The newcomer struck a stinker, negligently held the light to Craig's smoke, lit his own. "You're sure in one hell of a tight, mister," he commented casually.

"You telling me!" threw back the prisoner tautly.

"How come you hate Pomeroy's guts?"

Craig stiffened at the unexpected question. Without replying, he drew on his cigarette, eyeing the other closely.

"Maybe he ran you out of San Marcos County," suggested the deputy.

Craig laughed, without humor.

"For murdering Tom Waxman," added Harper.

The prisoner's features stiffened, but still he said nothing.

"Suspicion of murder and armed robbery," murmured the deputy. "You'll be lucky to dodge the rope, mister. And a life term in Yuma ain't my idea of Paradise. Wal, no one can claim you ain't guilty—guilty as hell."

"You're a liar!" snapped Craig.

Harper smiled genially. "Prove it!" he challenged.

Craig jumped up from the bench, began pacing with quick, jerky strides. "I've got no proof." He swung to face his interrogator. "If I spilled my guts, you'd laugh out loud."

"I kin always use a laugh," returned the deputy mildly.

The prisoner hesitated, then dropped back again onto the

bench, sat shoulders slumped, lips locked. *Why talk?* he asked himself hopelessly. No one, least of all a lawman, would believe his crazy story. He was sunk to the neck in a quicksand of circumstantial evidence, and now nothing on God's green earth could save him.

Harper broke a silence that was becoming oppressive. "Wal, maybe you'd answer a few questions," he suggested.

Craig shrugged.

The deputy pulled out the letter from Waxman's wife. "Why did you tip us off?" he wanted to know.

"To stop another killing," said Craig.

"Or make trouble for a lawman?"

"Lawman, hell!" barked Craig. "Pomeroy rods the stage-coach bandits. Waxman went to him for help—and signed his own death warrant."

Harper silently digested this, then he commented quietly, "That's hard to take, mister. Maybe a little proof would ease it down."

"I've got no proof," admitted the prisoner bitterly. "Evidence aplenty—unsupported evidence. Frosty Freeman beefed Waxman, on Pomeroy's orders. I was a witness. Frosty and Pomeroy are like that." He held up his right hand, two fingers together.

"Frosty Freeman!" murmured Harper. "He's dodging a federal warrant right now." He grinned cheerfully at the prisoner. "How in thunder did you get tangled in this mess?"

Craig hunched on the bench, eyeing the other doubtfully. Likely this affability was all a trick, he thought, to tighten the noose about his own neck. Then he found himself telling the whole story, at first slowly, then speeding up until words spilled from his lips in a forceful, fervent stream.

When he was through, he inquired glumly, "You ever heard a more loco yarn? I'm not figuring you'll swallow it—no sensible man would. But it's gospel, every word."

Harper grinned. "Sure sounds crazy," he admitted; "so doggoned crazy I can't figure you dreaming it up. Pomeroy now, would claim you been chewing locoweed."

"And what's to prove the sidewinder wrong?" demanded the prisoner hopelessly. "All you got is my word, and that sure ain't worth a shuck around here."

"Is that surprising?" inquired Harper mildly. He ran blunt fingers through his coppery hair. "There's been some funny stories percolating out of San Marcos County. Pomeroy's law enforcement record stinks, but that don't say he's crooked. How in creation we gonna prove he triggered Waxman's murder?"

"Loose me!" came back Craig promptly. "I tip you off when the next job's planned. You round up the pack and I'd stake my saddle someone squawks and ties Pomeroy in."

"Some might claim that's one slick way of acing out of the hoosegow," came back Harper, with a lazy smile.

"It's one way to corral Pomeroy."

"You figure McCloud would drop charges?"

Craig, remembering the superintendent's lean, hard features and cold eyes, smiled with drab humor. "Not McCloud," he said.

"Any pard who'd put up bail?"

"None nearer than San Antone."

"Then you're stuck," said the deputy.

His gawky form unwound as he straightened. "Guess I gotta chew on this a while," he decided, and stood eyeing the prisoner benevolently. "I'd say, Craig that you either got Ananias shaded or you're a plumb unlucky man."

XVI

SHERIFF KIRBY, whose bailiwick embraced Mineral County, was a waspish old-timer who walked with a limp, the legacy of a bullet wound, which men claimed had permanently curdled his disposition. The wrinkled skin stretched over his eroded features had the texture of old parchment, a graying handlebar moustache curved down on each side of a rat-trap mouth and his eyes were faded from long staring into sunglare. But his rep was as clean as a hound's tooth.

Following the U.S. deputy's interrogation of Burt Craig, the two lawmen were chewing the case over in Kirby's office. Harper lazily drew on a smoke.

"Wal, Limpy," he drawled, "what do you think of the hombre's recital?"

"A mess of hogwash!" grunted Kirby.

"Pomeroy's rep's none too good."

"Could be Jack Pomeroy did get too rich too quick," agreed the sheriff reluctantly.

"And you ain't asking how?"

"I got plenty to keep me busy in Mineral County, without sticking my snout into that gent's affairs," returned Kirby bleakly.

"Supposing—just supposing, Craig told a straight story?"

"Supposing you quit supposing," snapped the sheriff. "Straight story!" He sniffed. "Warn't he caught with his pants down? The lobo's as guilty as hell. I'd say he's good for a ten-year stretch, fifteen if Judge Markham's ulcers chance to be acting up."

"And Pomeroy gets away with murder," said Harper softly.

"You got no proof, nothing but Craig's say-so, which ain't worth a barrel of shucks."

For a while, Harper drew on his smoke, absorbing this, then threw back, "I got a sneaking hunch the maverick's on the up and up." He held up a hand as Kirby opened his mouth to speak. "Forget I'm loco and get the whole picture. There's been holdup trouble in San Marcos Country for months—it's the one sore spot on the whole danged Overland stage route between Kansas City and 'Frisco. Your county's clean, every county's clean, all but Pomeroy's. How come? That bustard's getting a payoff. You know it—I know it. Can we prove it? Not on your life."

While Kirby sat smoking imperturbably, the deputy paused to roll another cigarette. "Butterfield rings the Pinkerton outfit in," he continued, "and their man Waxman's murdered—just as soon as Pomeroy wises up as to his identity. Hell, it's plain as plowed ground that Pomeroy ordered the killing." He touched a light to his smoke. "Waxman was rodding the law, just like you and me; now he's buzzard bait." He leveled a long finger at the sheriff. "And you sit there, dumb as a cigar store Injun, and stomach it."

"Ain't nothing I can do," asserted Kirby irritably. "Craig

stays in the stir unless McCloud quashes charges, and it's a sure thing that sanctimonious son will buck at that, after Craig's bunch beefed three of his boys."

"With Craig locked up we're at a dead end; loose him, he'll work with us and we'll round up the whole gang."

"Loose the lobo," grunted Kirby, "and he'll streak for the border so fast his axles'll smoke."

"You game to gamble?"

"Ain't no gamble, it's a sure thing. What's more, I let him out and McCloud would have my badge quicker'n hell could scorch a feather."

Harper slacked, eyes closed, considering this. His lips began to curve in a slow smile. "You know, Limpy," he drawled, "the law says I got a prior claim on that prisoner. Uncle Sam wants the hombre for accessory to murder while looting the U.S. mail. That's a federal offense. Now, if I sign for the body, you're in the clear. McCloud's got no squawk. Uncle Sam's satisfied. I leave here a happy man."

"Now I know you're as crazy as a coon," expostulated Kirby. "You mislay the jasper on the trail to Tucson, he skeedaddles, you lose your badge and likewise your rep. Gordammit Brick, you're gambling on a busted flush."

"I keep remembering Waxman, cut down and left for the coyotes," said Harper slowly, "and thinking next time it'll be me—or you—with the likes of Pomeroy on the loose. Get busy on them transfer papers, Limpy—I'm going for broke."

The light of a new day had begun to sift into Craig's cell, graying his form stretched on the bench, when the complaint of gritty hinges stirred him into wakefulness. Bleary-eyed, he raised to a sitting position and blinked at the elongated form of U.S. Deputy Harper.

"Shake a leg, mister," said Harper crisply.

Still half drugged by sleep, the prisoner wearily reached for his boots. Outlined in the doorway, the jailor stood watching stolidly while Harper snapped handcuffs onto the prisoner's wrists.

Grasping that he had somehow passed into the deputy's custody, Craig followed Harper's lanky form down the passageway. Outside, two saddle horses were tied to a post of a roofed runway, beyond which loomed the courthouse.

Harper gave his prisoner a boost into the saddle, mounted himself and reached for the dangling reins of Craig's mount. At a walk, he rounded an angle of the courthouse and they emerged upon a twisted street squeezed between broken ridges, still almost obscured by the clinging mists of dawn.

They rode south, traversing a desolate monotony of broken hills, following a wagon road that snaked through gloomy canyons, coiled around the flanks of towering buttes. Noon was nearing when they topped a ridge and Harper drew rein, pointing ahead. "Tucson!" he volunteered, and added offhand, "A whoop and a holler from the border."

Humorlessly, Craig inquired, "My next jail?"

"Yep," said Harper, "on a federal charge—accessory to murder."

"Waxman?"

The deputy nodded.

Craig raised his shoulders helplessly. "I was there, but I never had a hand in it."

"Save it for the jury," advised Harper, and raised his reins. They drifted downgrade, rode out of the glare into the comparative coolness of a shadowed gulch. Midway along the gulch, water seeped up from some underground source and pooled among mossy boulders.

"Guess we noon here," decided Harper. He checked his mount and peeled out of leather. Craig followed suit. While Harper watered the ponies and slacked their cinches, Craig moved restlessly around, easing cramped limbs. Before sundown, he considered drearily, he'd be back in a cell, with nothing ahead but years of confinement or a spot in boothill. He was as good as convicted before he ever entered the courtroom. His one chance of clearing himself lay in accomplishing what he'd first set out to do: gather evidence that would convict Pomeroy and Frosty Freeman. Now that chance had vanished.

Harper yawned and flopped down against a boulder. "All-night poker sessions never did agree with me." He grinned. "Sure could use a little shut-eye."

Craig hunkered nearby, listlessly eyeing the cropping

horses, the placid pool, birds darting through shafts of sunlight. His glance fell on the deputy. Harper had dropped off to sleep, jaw sagging. The smooth wooden butt of his six-gun, protruding from the holster, drew Craig's eyes like a magnet. Get hold of that gun, he reflected, and he was as good as free. This was likely his last chance to make a break. Maybe he'd tangle his spurs, but what did he have to lose? Slowly, stealthily, he began to ease closer to the dozing lawman, wrists extended as far apart as possible to prevent a giveaway clink's disturbing the deputy. Nerves taut, sweat beading his brow, he reached. Harper, eyes closed, continued to breathe rhythmically.

The fingers of Craig's right hand closed on the polished butt of the .45. In a flash, he jerked the weapon clear, jumped backward, thumbing the hammer. Harper awoke with a start—and stared into the black muzzle of the gun.

"Stretch!" gritted the prisoner.

The lanky deputy slowly pushed his arms shoulder-high, eyes fixed on the gun.

"Drop that belt," directed Craig, his voice hoarse with strain, "and no trouble—I'd sure hate to plug you."

"I never argue with a pointed gun," drawled the other, and slipped the buckle of his gunbelt.

"Toss me the key to these damned cuffs."

In no haste, the deputy dipped into a pocket, brought out a stubby key and threw it carelessly toward Craig.

"Now back aways!"

Harper rose lazily and moved away from the gunbelt.

The prisoner scooped up the key with his left hand. Covering the tall deputy while unlocking the cuff that circled his right wrist proved to be no easy task. He could have sworn he read amusement in Harper's eyes as he fumbled with the key. Finally, the cuff clicked open and dropped away.

Arms uncoupled, he buckled on the gunbelt, began to move crabwise toward the grazing ponies, the handcuffs dangling from his left wrist.

"Where d'you figure you're going?" drawled the deputy.

"To finish a job in San Marcos County," threw back Craig.

"You sure better work fast," retorted Harper; "I'll be biting your dust." His good-humored tolerance as he stood watching his escaping prisoner tighten the ponies' cinches puzzled the Texan. It was hard to figure how such an easy-going cuss could hold a badge. "I'll tie your dun a mile or so back on the trail," said Craig, mounting.

"Sure obliged," returned his former captor gravely.

Harper lowered his arms, stood watching the getaway until rising dust blotted the two cantering ponies from view. For a lawman who had just lost a prisoner through sheer carelessness he seemed strangely unperturbed. He settled down, back propped against the boulder as before, and rolled a smoke. This he reduced to a butt and had almost consumed another when a rider on a sweated pony came up the gulch at a fast pace. Curbing his mount in a flurry of dust, he stepped out of leather and stood glaring at the complacent deputy.

"So you went thru with it, you doggoned hammerhead," he spluttered. "Now you not only lost your rep, but your hoss and gunbelt too."

"The hoss will be tied a mile back on the trail," drawled Harper, "and I'll donate the gunbelt. He rode north!"

"You telling me!" growled Kirby. "I 'most roasted laying all spraddled out, waiting for the bustard when he hit south for the border."

"You guessed wrong, Limpy," consoled the deputy. "Like I said, Craig's okay. Ain't he proved it? I'm staking my saddle he'll deliver. Now take the weight off your legs and cool off afore you collect my dun."

The sheriff sank down beside him, brought out his corncob pipe and stuffed the bowl. "I'm still claiming you made a fool play when you allowed that hombre to grab your gun," he grumbled. "The lobo coulda salivated you."

"Like hell he could," grinned the lanky deputy, "there warn't a bean on the wheel. Anyways, I always pack a replacement." He dipped into a boot top and brought out a stubby .41 Remington derringer.

"Slick as a greased hog!"

Harper chuckled. "Just careful! That one bet I figured it good business to copper."

XVII

WHEN HE emerged from the gulch, pounding along the backtrail, Craig reined his hard-breathing mount down to a jog trot. His getaway had been so sudden, and unexpected, that even now it was difficult to realize that he was free. He couldn't have made his escape at a better spot either, he reflected. Likely no one would pass along that lonely trail for hours, maybe days. The gawky, easy-going U.S. deputy was afoot and unarmed. By the time he'd legged through the heat and collected his mount, he, Craig, would be lost in the hills. Absently, he lifted Harper's single-action Colt out of the holster, flicked open the loading gate and swung out the cylinder to check the loads—and stiffened with the shock of surprise. The gun was empty. For a long moment he stared at the cylinder, as implications crowded his brain. There was only one answer: Harper *wanted* him to escape. It was plain now that the deputy believed the story he had told in the cell, fantastic though it must have appeared, and decided to give him another chance to make good. It seemed incredible, but there was no other way to explain the empty gun and Harper's failure to call what he knew was a monumental bluff.

Sobered now, the Texan checked his mount by a storm-blasted juniper. He loaded the gun from the stolen belt, then stepped out of the saddle and wrapped the reins of Harper's dun around the twisted trunk. Then he unlocked his remaining cuff, jangling from his left wrist, and hung the manacles on the horn, the key in place.

Angling away from the wagon road, he headed into the desolate hills, working northeast, in which direction he figured Cushman lay.

The countyseat slept beneath a glittering canopy of stars when Craig's buckskin jogged into town. Saddle-sore and dust-grayed, Craig drifted past the dim bulk of the courthouse, empty plankwalks and shuttered stores. Darkness enveloped Main Street, except where yellow shafts of light streamed from saloons and flowed over saddle horses standing hipshot outside. The silence was unbroken except for the occasional rasp of a gritty batwing, a snatch of talk or burst of hoarse laughter from a saloon.

Now that he'd arrived at his destination, the escaped prisoner fought a growing feeling of impotence. Just what could he do now? he wondered. The most likely place to locate the outlaws was at their former stamping ground—the canyon in the Mesquito Hills—but his mount was too jaded to carry him much further that night. He had to move fast. He had one more day, at the most, to deliver before Harper —and less understanding deputies—closed in. How in thunder could a man dig up enough evidence to convict Pomeroy in two days?

Checking at a trough to water his mount, he chewed on the problem—and found no answer.

Across the street loomed the square bulk of Steiner's Mercantile. Its windows were darkned, but a light showed in the rear of the store. Thought of the reform group the merchant headed and the five thousand dollar reward it had put up entered his mind—and sparked an idea. He reined across the street and glanced through one of the front windows. Light from a lamp suspended from the ceiling bathed the form of a compact, shirtsleeved man busy at a desk beyond the laden shelves and sweep of counters. Could be the hombre was Steiner.

A narrow alley divided the store from the adjoining building. Craig walked the buckskin down it, emerged beside a loading platform. From the picture, a sliding door gave admittance to the rear of the store. It was ajar.

He stepped down, tied his mount to an upright of the platform, climbed onto it. Easing back the door, he found himself in a huge storeroom. Light glimmered beyond a further doorway, half open. He crossed the storeroom, stepped through the doorway.

A blocky-built man with bushy iron-gray hair was hunched at a rolltop desk, pencil in hand, working on a stack of invoices.

His head came around with a jerk at Craig's appearance. "You Steiner?" inquired the fugitive.

If the merchant was startled, he gave no sign of it as he weighed his visitor's trail-stained form.

"I am!" he admitted. "Who are you?" The brusque tone was that of a man accustomed to command.

"The moniker's Burt Craig."

"Well, Craig, what do you want?" An itch of impatience lay on Steiner's tone.

"To earn that five thousand your reform committee put up, for conviction of the stagecoach gang."

"And exposure of public officials believed to be working with the bandits," added the merchant crisply.

"Such as Sheriff Pomeroy?"

"If Pomeroy is implicated."

"He's implicated—up to his neck," returned Craig grimly. "Wal, I can deliver."

"What makes you think so?" inquired the other, with awakening interest.

"I ride with the gang."

Steiner twirled his pencil with blunt fingers, studying the Texan. "Well," he commented finally, faint contempt tinging his tone, "I suppose every man has his price: Judas' was thirty pieces of silver."

"Guess you got me sized up wrong, mister," bit back Craig. "Sure I can use the dinero, but this is a payoff—for a holdup and a murder." The merchant reached, swept several catalogs off the seat of a chair beside the desk. "Sit down and tell me about it," he invited, more cordial now.

Craig plunked down and began to tell of the loss of his stake, his meeting with Waxman, his alliance with the gang under an assumed name and the cold-blooded murder of the Pinkerton man. "I know Pomeroy runs with the pack," he concluded, "but I lack evidence that will hold up in court. To get it, can I bank on your help?"

"To the limit!" Steiner assured him forcefully.

"If it means facing hot lead?"

The merchant smiled frostily. "Craig, I'm no stranger to trouble; neither are the men who back me. We pioneered this territory, made it safe for four-flushers like Pomeroy. I peddled my goods from a pack pony among isolated ranches, trusting to guile and a gun to escape marauding

Apaches and renegade Mexicans. When law finally prevailed we put our guns away—but we've kept them oiled."

"That sure sounds good to me," Craig assured him. "Now here's my plan: the gang holes up in a blind canyon in the Mesquito Hills. Block the mouth of that canyon and you got 'em bottled up. Frosty Freeman beefed Waxman. Frosty's bad right through and tougher than a basket of snakes. Could be he won't talk, but there's others who'd spill their guts to sidestep a hanging. And I gamble they'd implicate Pomeroy."

"The idea sounds practical," mused Steiner. "How many men would you need to handle the job?"

"A dozen guns would be plenty."

The merchant fingered his chin, considering. "I could gather a dozen armed men by sundown tomorrow," he decided.

"Fine!" Craig strove to strain the excitement out of his voice. In twenty-four hours, he reflected, Pomeroy's goose would be cooked and he'd be in the clear, with a fat stake that would enable him to go ahead with his deal for Jensen's spread. Seemed his luck had finally changed.

"Listen!" he said. "You get your men together. I been . . . away. At sunup I'll ride out and check on the canyon. The bunch may be away on a job. If they're in the canyon I'll be back at sundown. We can clean 'em up before the sun rises."

"You forget Pomeroy?" questioned Steiner. It was apparent that the sheriff's conviction took first place in the merchant's mind.

"We'll get enough on that bustard to hang him," promised Craig confidently.

"That's essential! Convicting or killing a bunch of border riffraff means little if their leader goes free," insisted Steiner. His clenched fist pounded the desk. "Pomeroy must be convicted. The reputation of this county is becoming a stench throughout the entire territory." He rose and extended a hand. "Good luck, Craig! We'll be expecting you tomorrow after sundown. My men will be ready. You'll do more than earn a bounty; you'll earn the thanks of every decent man in San Marcos County."

Outside again, the Texan mounted and threaded through the alley back to Main Street. He headed the pony down street, out of town. Reaction to the long day's ride, the excitement of the escape, the strain of anxiety, had set in. His limbs seemed leaded, his eyes ached from sunglare, his whole body sagged from fatigue. When the last outlying shack had faded into the night behind him, he pulled off the stage road, dismounted amid scrubby brush. Tiredly, he slacked the buckskin's cinches, draped the reins around his left wrist, stretched out and, near exhaustion, sank into deep sleep.

XVIII

JAKE was the first to sight the fugitive when he rode into the canyon. "Jehoshaphat!" he exclaimed. "Craig!"

The Texan stepped out of leather and stood looking around. Five outlaws, he tallied; so he'd guessed right. Everyone but himself had escaped from the gold shipment fracas and they were all holed up here. Two members of Smoky's gang, slapping cards on a spread blanket, gave him no more than a glance. A third, cleaning a Winchester, eyed him curiously. Jake lumbered toward him, and Frosty, edgy as always, approached with quick steps.

"Where you been hiding out?" demanded Frosty, pale eyes flicking over the newcomer.

"In the hoosegow at Mineral King," Craig told him shortly. "This big bustard"—he jerked his head toward Jake—"quit me cold when a slug downed my hoss. Yesterday, a U.S. deputy collected me to face federal charges. I grabbed his gun and made a break."

"U.S. marshals ain't that careless," bit back the thin-faced renegade.

"You calling me a liar?" snapped Craig. Their glances locked and he braced for flaming gunplay as Jake hastily shuffled clear. But, to his surprise, Frosty ignored the challenge. "Wal, I guess you were lucky, doggoned lucky," he admitted reluctantly. "Pomeroy sent word. He craved to see you—pronto—if you showed."

"What would Pomeroy want with me?"

"You forget the homicide charge, for beefing Brazos?"

"The charge was disturbing the peace!"

Frosty smiled sourly. "Maybe that law and order committee thinks different and is raising a stink."

If Steiner's committee was making trouble, reflected the Texan, the merchant would have mentioned it. Something else was itching the sheriff. At that, things could not have worked out better. Here was a ready-made excuse for riding back to town and alerting Steiner that the bandits were in the canyon. He'd find some reason for sticking around Cushman and lead the cleanup bunch back that night. Concealing his elation, he grumbled, "Now I got to hit leather again!" He set a boot in the stirrup. Frosty grabbed a rein. "Hold it!" said the outlaw sharply.

"What's itching you now?" Craig's tone brittled with impatience.

"You got company—Jake and me."

"I don't crave company, least of all Jake's."

Frosty's bony fingers tightened on the rein. "You got no choice, Craig." There was a quality in the bitter-eyed bandit's tone that telegraphed trouble. The Texan's angry eyes focused on Frosty's thin features, switched to Jake. The burly outlaw's right hand was clamped on his gun butt and there was no mistaking the eager anticipation in his bloodshot eyes. Aching for an excuse to draw, thought Craig. There was something here he didn't understand, something under the surface. He wouldn't have a show if shooting started—not in this nest of outlaws. What was more, trouble was the last thing he craved right now. He just had to get back to town, with or without these two hardcases. When they arrived, he'd find some means to ditch them and contact Steiner.

He shrugged and returned indifferently, "Have it your way."

When the three rode out of the canyon, the outlaws rode on either side of Craig, almost, he reflected, as though he were a prisoner. Puzzled, he tried to account for this queer turn of events.

It had nothing to do with Brazos' shooting, he was convinced of that. The sheriff had plainly given orders that he was to be escorted to town. That meant Pomeroy had an urgent reason for confronting him. What reason could there be? He curbed an impulse to fire questions. The smartest play, he decided, was to button up. When he heard what Pomeroy had to say he'd know how to play his cards. Meanwhile he just had to sweat it out, because any sign of anxiety or nervousness would increase whatever suspicions the calloused pair riding at his stirrups nursed. But he couldn't down a growing premonition that now, right on the threshold of success, he was about to tangle his spurs.

It was near noon when they jogged over the ruts of Main Street; Cushman drowsed under a blanket of heat.

Outside the courthouse the three wheeled to the rail. When they trudged up the brick steps, Craig noted that Frosty dropped to the rear. Every instinct told him he was under suspicion. Why? he reflected, with gnawing frustration. What trick of fate had tripped him now, when all he needed was twenty-four hours?

The sheriff's office was empty except for Pomeroy when they filed through the doorway. Seated at his desk, the sheriff spun around at sound of their entry, jerked to his feet. For the first time, reflected Craig, the bland smile was lacking, the smooth brow was etched with worry and uncertainty clouded the brassy blue eyes. The sheriff was scared, registered Craig, scared stiff.

He checked an arm's length from the lawman and inquired curtly, "Wal?"

"Who in hell are you?" exploded Pomeroy.

For an instant the unexpected question held the Texan tongue-tied. Then he threw back, "Lester Collins, who else?"

"You're lying!" snarled the sheriff. "Lester Collins was cornered by a posse and cut down near Marlburg, Texas, eight months back."

Craig knew he couldn't bluff this one through. He'd overlooked that hazard when he had assumed the wanted bank robber's identity—that the fugitive might have been killed or captured. Pomeroy had plainly been in touch with the Texas sheriff who'd issued the warrant. And there was no out. Impulsively, he stabbed for the gun in his holster—

and hard fingers from behind latched onto his wrist. "Simmer down, mister, or you're cold meat," advised Frosty's grating accents. With a leaden feeling of helplessness, Craig felt the gun being lifted out of his holster.

Pomeroy stood staring at him, gnawing at his underlip. "Just what kind of whizzer are you running?" he demanded finally.

Craig stood poker-faced, mentally cursing his own impulsiveness. Dabbing for the gun had been a clear giveaway.

"You another Pinkerton dick?" fumed the sheriff.

"Nope!"

"Wal, strip!"

The Texan stood unmoving. The hard muzzle of a six-gun jabbed into his backbone. "Do like the sheriff says," directed Frosty's cold voice from the rear. "Or do I blow a hole through your guts?"

Craig dropped onto a chair and began yanking off his boots. Sox, pants followed, until he sat stark naked, his duds piled on the floor before him. Pomeroy picked up the articles of clothing, one by one, turned out the pockets of the vest and pants, fingered the linings, hunting a hidden badge. Finally, with mounting impatience, he ripped off the sweatband of the hat—with no more luck.

"Maybe the coyote's too slick to pack a badge," commented Frosty.

"Hogwash!" exclaimed Craig. He came to his feet and reached for his pants. Unexpectedly, in a spat of anger, the sheriff swung a bunched fist at his unprotected belly. Taken unaware, the Texan had no chance to parry. He jackknifed with an agonized gasp as the fist sank home. Pomeroy's right leg drew back. He aimed a swift kick at the other's bent head. Clutching, Craig's hands grabbed the sheriff's polished boot top. He twisted with all his remaining strength. Pomeroy spilled sideways, arms flailing as he strove to maintain balance. His heavy body cannoned into the desk, bounced off. Craig loosed his grip of the leg, flung himself at the staggering lawman. His fingers fastened onto the sheriff's throat—and Frosty's six-gun chopped down on the back of his head. His grip slackened. He collapsed, limp as a wet sack, dropped and lay unmoving.

Frosty dropped his gun back into the holster. Jake stared, broad features creased with amusement. Pomeroy stood tenderly caressing his throat and glaring at the naked form on the floor.

When the sheriff spoke, his voice was hoarse. "Guess this cuss is too dangerous to have around."

Jake yanked an ugly dagger-like knife from a sheath at his belt, ran a callused thumb along its edge. "I'll take care of it." He grinned, and bent over the slack form.

"Not here!" barked Pomeroy, with harassed irritation. "Ain't I in trouble enough already?" He turned to Frosty. "Get him out of town. Beef him back in the hills, any place so I never see or hear of the bustard again."

"It'll be a pleasure," grated the bitter-eyed outlaw.

Still half stunned, Craig heard the talk as though from a great distance. He stirred and groaned as a sharp-toed riding boot thudded into his bare torso. Frosty's acrid tones reached his ears. "On your feet, you double-crossing skunk. Git into them duds."

Brain still numbed from the blow, the Texan levered painfully erect, teetered to a chair and collapsed upon it. Close-watched by three pairs of hard eyes, he began listlessly yanking on his pants. . . .

Three riders threaded through rolling foothills far from Cushman.

XIX

DUST FOGGED as the string of three riders dropped down the crumbling banks of a dry creek in the foothills and their ponies' hooves stirred the powdery bed. Half-blinded, Craig unconsciously checked his mount. Tailing him through the choking haze, Jake's mount blundered into his buckskin. The burly outlaw ripped out an oath, pushed up beside the prisoner. Craig's head turned as the renegade's form loomed, indistinct, at his stirrup. Sight of the gun bumping Jake's hip, within arm's length, sparked inspiration, born of desperation, in the Texan's mind. Before the slow-thinking outlaw grasped his intent, his left hand dabbed out, snatched the .45 out of leather. Jake's head turned in startled reaction. As it swiveled, Craig swung hard at the outlaw's heavy features with a sweeping backarm blow. The barrel of the Colt took the burly Jake squarely on the mouth. Craig heard the crunch of smashed teeth, a strangled yell of agony, as the slamming gun knocked the renegade backward out of the saddle.

Ahead, Frosty had whirled his pony. Vaguely, through thick-floating dust, Craig glimpsed the forms of horse and rider as the wiry outlaw spurred at him. Ducking low, he switched Jake's .45 to his right hand and thumbed the hammer. Through the murk, Frosty's gun spewed flame and thunder, got the buckskin. As it went down, Craig kicked free of the stirrups, rolled clear of the threshing hooves of the dying animal. The dust haze thickened. Half choked and blinded, Craig lay and loosed lead, his target no more than a gray ghost in the gloom. The purloined gun thundered and bucked, thundered and bucked again, and again. In reply, fire lanced from Frosty's .45. Raising on one knee, Craig loosed a final shot at the flash. When the hammer descended for the sixth time it yielded no more than a metallic click. He was through; now Frosty could cut him down at leisure. The dust began to settle, making his crouched form a plain target. But Frosty had quit throwing lead, too. Staring through reddened eyes, Craig saw that the wiry outlaw's form was slacked across his pony's withers, gun hand dangling, empty. Gripping his empty gun, Craig straightened and cautiously eased closer. Braced to club the renegade, he reached with his left hand, grabbed a limp arm and yanked. The inert form slowly slid down, thudded to the ground at his feet, flabby as a rag doll. Frosty was dead.

The Texan quickly slipped the buckle of the outlaw's gunbelt, wrenched it off and swung it around his own middle. Then he stood, breathing hard, striving to adjust to the realization that he had cheated death. He remembered Jake, and his head pivoted, searching through the thinning haze.

The outlaw was huddled against the far bank, a bandanna, dripping blood, wadded against mouth and nose. Nearby stood his bay. Keeping an eye on the burly rider, Craig plugged fresh loads into the Colt. Gun in hand, he plodded through ankle-deep dust toward the outlaw. In no mood for kindliness, he booted the groaning Jake to his feet. Big form sagging, dabbing at his bloody mouth and mashed nose, Jake made no resistance when Craig stripped off his gunbelt and knife. All the fight seemed to have oozed out of him. Craig propelled him back to his saddle horse, and strode over to Frosty's pony. He mounted, ignoring the crumpled remains of the bitter-eyed bandit. The coyotes could pick Frosty's bones, he decided, just as they had picked Waxman's. Jake slumped against his mount. "Hit leather!" barked Craig. "I'm taking you back to town," he announced with tight satisfaction. "You make trouble and I'll sure enjoy working on you with that Arkansas toothpick you craved to use on me." Lifelessly, Jake hauled into the saddle. . . .

Followed by the curious glances of long-skirted lady shoppers and sales clerks, the Texan propelled the burly outlaw down an aisle of Steiner's rambling emporium. When they neared the rear of the store, Steiner stepped out of his office.

"What brought you back so soon?" he inquired sharply, then tautened with shock at sight of Jake's battered countenance. The outlaw's smashed nose was smeared across his broad features like a bloody blob of putty; his swollen lips gaped, revealing yellow snags of broken teeth.

"This man needs a doctor," snapped Steiner.

"The bustard earned worse," Craig told the merchant curtly. He eyed a clerk, gaping nearby. "We got to talk—in private," he told the merchant.

Steiner nodded, led the way back into the dim recesses of the storeroom and closed the door behind them.

"Well?" he inquired brusquely. Craig told how the sheriff had learned of his imposture and the events that followed, culminating with his breakaway in the creek bed on the fringe of the Mesquito Hills.

90

"You crave evidence to back my word," he wound up, "this big ox will talk and talk plenty." He nodded contemptuously at Jake's shambling form. "He's got a yellow streak a yard wide; it laps plumb around to his brisket bone."

Steiner stood listening intently and pulling at his chin. "Perhaps we should accost the sheriff right now," he suggested thoughtfully.

"Suits me," said the Texan, "but freeze onto this maverick. He's our ace in the hole. Pomeroy get a chance, he'll close his yap for keeps."

"The trouble is that we're shorthanded if difficulties should develop with Pomeroy and his deputies." The merchant frowned. "I sent word to a dozen members of the committee to meet here at sundown. I doubt if any have arrived yet. We'll see!" He headed for the door in the rear, threading through piled merchandise. Thrusting Jake ahead, Craig followed.

Steiner rolled the door back. Three weathered old-timers were gathered in a knot on the loading platform, trading talk.

"Things are moving faster than I anticipated," Steiner told them with a tight smile. He quickly related the gist of Craig's story. "Now," he concluded, "we must move before the sheriff learns he has been unmasked. I intend to arrest him, by force if necessary, and hold him until an emergency town meeting can be called."

"You're late, Carl," drawled one of the old-timers. "Pomeroy already beat it. I lamped the sidewinder boarding an eastbound stage when I rode in, an hour back. He was packing a carpet bag."

Pomeroy, reflected Craig, realized he had reached the end of the trail and was hightailing with what spoils he could salvage. The murder of two Pinkerton detectives— as he thought—would likely bring fast retribution. "An hour!" he interjected. "Stages stop at Wicker's Ford to change teams. We cut across country, we've still got time to head off that stage in the Mesquito Hills."

"Let's ride!" snapped Steiner. "I'd hate to have that skunk slip through our fingers now!"

The sun was dropping toward the Copperheads when five riders on sweated ponies drew rein in the cut where Tom Waxman's form had stiffened. Under Craig's direction, they rolled boulders across the ruts of the stage road. When they were through and their mounts concealed in the near-by arroyo, Steiner, his business suit dust-powdered, stood mopping his brow with a handkerchief that had once been white. "I've tackled many jobs," he commented with a wry smile, "but I never dreamed that holding up a stage would be among them."

"Don't take any chances," cautioned Craig. "Stick behind cover till I give word. If there's a Wells Fargo box on that stage the guard's liable to greet us with a bellyful of buckshot."

Scarcely had he spoken when the distant pistol-like crack of a whip reached their ears. Every man froze, listening. The rumble of approaching wheels grew louder.

"Duck!" ordered Craig. The posse scattered, dropping down behind boulders that cluttered the cut. Craig flattened behind the barricade. There was the usual pile-up of snorting, hoof-threshing horses. The cursing man on the box fought to straighten them out as Craig jumped up. To his relief there was no shotgun guard.

From behind rocks on either side, the four remaining possemen emerged, guns ready. The driver's glance lit on Cushman's leading merchant, in a rumpled store suit, a Winchester in his hands. "Steiner!" he gasped, and almost swallowed his chaw.

"Pomeroy aboard?" yelled Craig.

"Sure is," threw back the driver. "Suffering buzzard's whelps, what in creation's afoot?"

The possemen were approaching the coach. Steiner threw open a door and stood back, rifle leveled. "Out, Pomeroy!" he shouted.

Standing by the leaders' heads, Craig saw the sheriff's dark-clad form emerge from the coach. Grasping the handle of a bulging carpet bag in one hand, he stepped down and stood in the elongated shadow of the stage. Behind him, faces were white-blobbed against the windows.

Pomeroy looked down at the compact Steiner, holding

a Winchester on him, with frowning perplexity. "This must be a joke," he said, and laughed uneasily.

"Nope!" the merchant told him curtly. "It's the end—for you. We're taking you back to Cushman, Pomeroy, to face a flock of charges, among them murder."

"Murder! You must be loco," expostulated the sheriff.

"Remember Waxman?" shouted Craig.

Pomeroy swung around. When he focused on the man he thought dead his jaw dropped and his eyes distended with the shock of surprise. In panicky reaction, he snatched at the butt of a gun holstered below his hip. Steiner's Winchester spat red death. The report of the gun ringing in his ears, Craig saw the dark-clad form abruptly stiffen, then slowly fold up and collapse in a shapeless heap beside the stage.

Just like Waxman, thought the Texan, and began rolling boulders aside. "Get going!" he shouted to the driver.

The bearded ancient on the box released the brake, shaking his head in bewilderment. What a hell of a story he'd have to tell at the next stop, thought Craig.

When the heavy Concord rolled on, the five gathered around Pomeroy's limp form, the carpet bag lying beside it.

"Holy Moses," muttered a posseman, "I never figured it would end thisaway."

Steiner ignored him. "Check that bag, Craig!" he directed.

The Texan dropped on one knee, opened up the carpet bag, and dipped inside. He threw out a clean shirt, two folded yellow bandannas. Then his fingers fastened on a buckskin pouch. It jingled when he dropped it to the ground. Another fat pouch followed, then wads of greenbacks. There seemed to be no end to the neat bundles of currency. Fascinated, the others stood silently watching the stack grow.

"The bustard was sure wallowing in velvet," commented one finally.

"He had a good collection system," said Steiner stonily and reached for one of the buckskin pouches. Removing a leather whang that secured its neck, he spilled a golden stream of double eagles onto a palm.

"And saving ways!" contributed another.

"I'd say he saved plenty—on a sheriff's salary," returned the merchant with an ironic smile. "If it weren't for Craig here, he'd still be saving."

XX

MISS WICKER was busy in the kitchen, pie-making, when Craig sauntered in. "Howdy!" he greeted offhand, dropped onto a chair and lifted the makin's from a vest pocket.

The girl swung around, arms floury, brown hair disheveled. "Just who are you?" she demanded, with a touch of belligerency.

"Lester Collins," he drawled. " 'Member, you had me arrested."

"Do you have to remind me?" she retorted. "I'll never forgive myself for that awful mistake. Tom Farnham, the deputy, started worrying about his bounty, telegraphed the Texas sheriff from Tucson and discovered Collins had been dead for months."

"So that's how Pomeroy wised up," murmured Craig.

"Every stage that goes through brings fresh rumors," continued the girl. "No one talks of anything but that awful sheriff and his villainy. They claim you are a Pinkerton man, a Wells Fargo detective, a deputy marshal working undercover, a robbery victim who was determined to expose Pomeroy. I surely would like to know the truth."

The Texan chuckled. "Wal, I guess a deputy marshal by the name of Harper spread the yarn that I was an undercover man—to ease me out of a jam I got into over in Mineral County. You crave the truth, I'm just what I claimed to be when you first fixed my head—Burt Craig, cowman, bound for Cushman to buy a ranch."

"A stubborn Texan," she returned with a faint smile, "who refused to quit."

"A loco maverick," corrected Craig with a grin, "hellbent to recover a looted stake."

"Well, did you?" she demanded crisply.

"With a bonus," he chuckled. "Five thousand smackers."

She became preoccupied with her pie-making. "I suppose you'll return to Texas now—a richer and wiser man."

He shrugged. "Maybe I'll stick around a while. Met Jensen in town. The deal for his Box J is still open."

"Well, what brought you back to Wicker's Ford?"

"You forgot my ring?"

"Oh!" she said abruptly. He sat eyeing her quizzically as she slowly wiped the flour off her hands and arms with a towel, and stepped into the adjoining room.

Returning, she handed him the ring without speaking.

"Sure is pretty," he commented, eyeing the blood-red ruby, circled by the glittering brilliants.

"It's beautiful!" she said softly.

"And I guess it belongs right there." He reached quickly, grabbed her left hand and slipped the ring on the third finger.

"Why, Burt Craig," she gasped. "Do you realize what that means?"

"Do you?" he threw back.

The glow in her eyes was sufficient answer.